THE HUSBANDS
OF EDITH

MORE WILDSIDE CLASSICS

THE HUSBANDS OF EDITH

GEORGE BARR McCUTCHEON

WILDSIDE PRESS

THE HUSBANDS OF EDITH

This edition published 2005 by Wildside Press, LLC.
www.wildsidepress.com

CHAPTER I

HUSBANDS AND WIFE.

Brock was breakfasting out-of-doors in the cheerful little garden of the Hôtel Chatham. The sun streamed warmly upon the concrete floor of the court just beyond the row of palms and oleanders that fringed the rail against which his *Herald* rested, that he might read as he ran, so to speak. He was the only person having *déjeuner* on the "terrace," as he named it to the obsequious waiter who always attended him. Charles was the magnet that drew Brock to the Chatham (that excellent French hotel with the excellent English name). It is beside the question to remark that one is obliged to reverse the English when directing a *cocher* to the Chatham. The Paris cabman looks blank and more than usually unintelligent when directed to drive to the Chatham, but his face radiates with joy when his fare is inspired to substitute Sha-*t'am*, with distinct emphasis on the final syllable. Then he cracks his whip and lashes his sorry nag, with passive appreciation of his own astuteness, all the way to the Rue Daunou. The street is so short that he almost invariably takes one to *it* instead of to the hotel itself. But one must say Sha-*t'am*!

Charles was standing, alert but pensive, quite near at hand, ready to replenish the bowl with honey (Brock was especially fond of it), but with his eyes cocked inquiringly, even eagerly, in the direction of an upstairs window across the court, beyond which a thoughtless guest of the establishment was making her toilette in blissful ignorance of the fact that the flimsy curtains were not tightly drawn. Brock had gone to the Chatham for years just because Charles was a fixture there. Charles spoke the most execrably picturesque English, served with a punctiliousness that savoured almost of the overbearing, and boasted that he had acquired the art of making American cocktails in the Waldorf during a five weeks' residence in the United States.

It was a lazy morning. Brock was happy. He was even interested when a porter came forth and unravelled a long roll of garden hose, with which he abruptly began to splash water upon the concrete surface of the court without regard for distance or direction. Moreover, he proceeded to water the palms at Brock's elbow, operating from a spot no less than twenty feet away. He likewise was casting inquiring glances at divers windows — few if any at the plants — until the faithful Charles restored him to earth by means of certain subdued injunctions and less moderate gesticulations, from which it could be readily gathered that "M'sieur was eating, not bathing." Whereupon the utterly uncrushed porter splashed water at right angles, much to Brock's relief, while all his fellow porters, free or engaged, took up the quarrel with rare disregard for cause or justice. A *femme de chambre*, from a convenient window, joined in the hubbub without in the least knowing what it was all about. Monsieur's comfort must be preserved: that seemed to be the issue in which, at once, all were united. "M'sieur will pardon the boy," apologised Charles in deepest humility, taking much for granted. "It will be very warm today. Your *serviette*, M'sieur — it is damp. Pardon!" He flew away and back with another napkin. "Of course, M'sieur, the Chatham is not the Waldorf," he announced deprecatingly. "*Parbleu*," beating himself on the forehead, "I forgot! M'sieur does not like the Waldorf. *Eh, bien*, Paris is not New York, no." Having sufficiently humbled Paris, he withdrew into the background, rubbing his hands as if he were cleansing them of something unsightly. Brock spread one of the buttered biscuits with honey and inwardly admitted that Paris was *not* New York.

He was a good-looking chap of thirty or thereabouts, an

American to the core — bright eyed, keen witted, smooth faced, virile. From boyhood's earliest days he had spent a portion of his summers in Europe. Two or three years of his life had been employed in the Beaux Arts — fruitful years, for Brock had not wasted his opportunities. He had gone in for architecture and building. Today he stood high among the younger men in New York — prosperous, successful, and a menace to the old cry that a son of the rich cannot thrive in his father's domain. Nowadays he came to the Old World for his breathing spells. He was able to combine dawdling and development without sacrificing one for the other, wherein lies the proof that his vacations were not akin to those taken by most of us.

The fortnight in Paris was to be followed by a week in St. Petersburg and a brief tour of Sweden and Norway. His stay in the gay city was drawing to a close. That very morning he expected to book for St. Petersburg, leaving in three days.

Suddenly his glance fell upon a name in the society column before him, "Roxbury Medcroft." His face lighted up with genuine pleasure. An old friend, a boon companion in bygone days, was this same Medcroft — a broad-minded, broad-gauged young Englishman who had profited by a stay of some years in the States. They had studied together in Paris and they had toiled together in New York. This is what he read: "Mr. and Mrs. Roxbury Medcroft, of London, are stopping at the Ritz, *en route* to Vienna. Mr. Medcroft will attend the meeting of Austrian Architects, to be held there next week, and, with his wife, will afterwards spend a fortnight in the German Alps, the guests of the Alfred Rodneys, of Seattle."

"Dear old Rox, I must look him up at once," mused Brock. "The Rodneys of Seattle? Never heard of 'em." He looked at his watch, signed his check, deposited the usual franc, acknowledged Charles's well practised smile of thanks, and pushed back his chair, his gaze travelling involuntarily toward the portals of the American bar across the court, just beyond the *concierge's* quarters. Simultaneously a tall figure emerged from the bar, casting eager glances in all directions, — a tall figure in a checked suit, bowler hat, white reindeer gloves, high collar, and grey spats. Brock came to his feet quickly. The monocle dropped from the other's eye, and his long legs carried him eagerly toward the American.

"Medcroft! Bless your heart! I was just on the point of looking you up at the Ritz. It's good to see you," Brock cried as they clasped hands.

"Of all the men and of all the times, Brock, you are the most opportune," exclaimed the other. "I saw that you were here and bolted my breakfast to catch you. These beastly telephones never work. Oh, I say, old man, have you finished yours?"

"Quite — but luckily I didn't have to bolt it. You're off for Vienna, I see. Sit down, Rox. Won't you have another egg and a cup of coffee? Do!"

"Thanks and no to everything you suggest. Wot you doing for the next half hour or so? I'm in a deuce of a dilemma and you've got to help me out of it." The Englishman looked at his watch and fumbled it nervously as he replaced it in his upper coat pocket. "That's a good fellow, Brock. You *will* be the ever present help in time of trouble, won't you?"

"My letter of credit is at your disposal, old man," said Brock promptly. He meant it. It readily may be seen from this that their friendship is no small item to be considered in the development of this tale.

"My dear fellow, that's the very thing I'm eager to thrust upon you — my letter of credit," exclaimed the other.

"What's that?" demanded Brock.

"I say, Brock, can't we go up to your rooms? Dead secret, you know. Really, old chap, I mean it. No one must get a breath of it. That's why I'm whispering. I'm not a lunatic, so don't stare like that. I'd do as much for you if the conditions were reversed."

"I dare say you would, Rox, but what the devil is it you want me to do?"

"Do I appear to be agitated?"

"Well, I should say so."

"Well, I *am*. You know how I loathe asking a favour of anyone. Besides, it's rather an extraordinary one I'm going to ask of you. Came to me in a flash this morning when I saw your name in the paper. Sort of inspiration, 'pon my word. I think Edith sees it the same as I, although I haven't had time to go into it thoroughly with her. She's ripping, you know; pluck to the very core."

Brock's face expressed bewilderment and perplexity.

"Won't you have another drink, old man?" he asked gently.

"Another? Hang it all, I haven't had one in a week. Come along. I must talk it all over with you before I introduce you to her. You must be prepared."

"Introduce me to whom?" demanded Brock, pricking up his ears. He was following Medcroft to the elevator.

"To my wife — Edith," said Medcroft, annoyed by the other's obtuseness.

"Does it require preparation for an ordeal so charming?" laughed Brock. He was recalling the fact that Medcroft had married a beautiful Philadelphia girl some years ago in London, a young lady whom he had never seen, so thoroughly expatriated had she become in consequence of almost a lifetime residence in England. He remembered now that she was rich and that he had sent her a ridiculously expensive present and a congratulatory cablegram at the time of the wedding. Also, it occurred to him that the Medcrofts had asked him to visit them at their shooting-box for several seasons in succession, and that their town house was always open to him. While he had not ignored the invitations, he had never responded in person. He began to experience twinges of remorse: Medcroft was such a good fellow!

The Londoner did not respond to the innocuous query. He merely stared in a preoccupied, determined manner at the succeeding *étages* as they slipped downward. At the fourth floor they disembarked, and Brock led the way to his rooms, overlooking the inner court. Once inside, with the door closed, he turned upon the Englishman.

"Now, what's up, Rox? Are you in trouble?" he demanded.

"Are we quite alone?" Medcroft glanced significantly at the transom and the half closed bathroom door. With a laugh, Brock led him into the bathroom and out, and then closed the transom.

"You're darned mysterious," he said, pointing to a chair near the window. Medcroft drew another close up and seated himself.

"Brock," he said, lowering his voice and leaning forward impressively, "I want you to go to Vienna in my place." Brock stared hard. "You are a godsend, old man. You're just in time to do me the greatest of favours. It's utterly impossible for me to go to Vienna as I had planned, and yet it is equally unwise for me to give up the project. You see, I've just got to be in London and Vienna at the same time."

"It will require something more than a stretch of the imagination to do that, old man. But I'm game, and my plans are such that they can be changed readily to oblige a friend. I shan't mind the trip in the least and I'll be only too happy to help you out! Gad, I thought by your manner that you were in some frightful difficulty. Have a cigaret."

"By Jove, Brock, you're a brick," cried Medcroft, shaking the other's hand vigorously. At the same time his face expressed considerable uncertainty and no little doubt as to the further welfare of his as yet partially divulged proposition.

"It's easy to be a brick, my boy, if it involves no more than the changing of a single letter in one's name. I'd like to attend the convention, anyway," said Brock amiably.

"Well, you see, Brock," said Medcroft lamely, "I fear you don't quite appreciate the situation. I want you to pose as Roxbury Medcroft."

"You — What do you mean?"

"I thought you'd find that a facer. That's just it: you are to go to Vienna as Roxbury Medcroft, not as yourself. Ha, ha! Ripping, eh?"

"'Pon my soul, Rox, you are not in earnest?"

"Never more so."

"But, my dear fellow —"

"You won't do it? That's what your tone means," in despair.

"It isn't that, and you know it. I've got nothing to lose. It's you that will have to suffer. You're known all over Europe. What will be said when the trick is discovered? Gad, man!"

"Then you will go?" with beaming eyes. "I knew it would appeal to you, as an American."

"What does it all mean?"

"It's all very simple, if one looks at it from the right angle, Brock. Up to last night, I was blissfully committed to the most delightful of outings, so to speak. At ten o'clock everything was changed. Mrs. Medcroft and I sat up all night discussing the situation with the messenger — my solicitor, by the way. The Vienna trip is out of the question, so far as I am concerned. It is of vital importance that I should return to London tonight, but is even more vitally important that the world should say that I am in Vienna. See what I mean?"

"No, I'm hanged if I do."

"What I have just heard from London makes me shudder to think of the consequences if I go on east tonight. I may as well tell you that there is a plot on foot to perpetrate a gigantic fraud against the people. The County Council is to be hoodwinked out and out into moving forward certain building projects, involving millions of the people's money. Our firm has opposed a certain band of grafters, and when I left England it was pretty well settled that we had blocked their game. They have learned of my proposed absence and intend to steal a march on us while I am away. Without assuming too much credit to myself, I may say that I, your old friend, Roxbury, I am the one man who has proved the real thorn in the sides of these scoundrels. With me out of the way, they feel that they can secure the adoption of all these infamous measures. My partners and the leaders on our side have sent for me to return secretly. They won't bring the matter to issue if they find that I've returned; it would be suicidal. Therefore it is necessary that we steal a march on 'em. I know the inside workings of the scheme. If I can steal back and keep under cover as an advisory chief, so to speak, we can well afford to let 'em rush the matter through, for then we can spring the coup and defeat them for good and all. But, don't you see, old man, unless they *know* that I've gone to Vienna they won't undertake the thing. That's why I'm asking you to go on to Vienna and pose as Roxbury Medcroft while I steal back to London and set the charge under these demmed bloodsuckers. Really, you know, it's a terribly serious matter, Brock. It means fortune and honour to me, as well as millions to the rate-payers of Greater London. All you've got to do is to register at the Bristol, get interviewed by the papers, attend one or two sessions of the convention, which lasts three days, and then go off into the mountains with the Rodneys — the society reporters will do the rest."

"With the Rodneys? My dear fellow, suppose that they

object to the substitution! Really, you know, it's not to be thought of."

"Deuce take it, man, the Rodneys are not to know that there has been a substitution. Perfectly simple, can't you see?"

"I'm damned if I do."

"What a stupid ass you are, Brock! The Rodneys have never laid eyes on me. They know of me as Edith's husband, that's all. They are to take you in as Medcroft, of course."

At this point Brock set up an emphatic remonstrance. He began by laughing his friend to scorn; then, as Medcroft persisted, went so far as to take him severely to task for the proposed imposition on the unsuspecting Rodneys, to say nothing of the trick he would play upon the convention of architects.

"I'd be recognised as an impostor," he said warmly, "and booted out of the convention. I shudder to think of what Mr. Rodney will do to me when he learns the truth. Why, Medcroft, you must be crazy. There will be dozens of architects there who know you personally or by sight. You —"

"My dear boy, if they don't see me there, they can't very well recognise me, can they? If necessary, you can affect an illness and stay away from the sessions altogether. Give a statement to the press from the privacy of the sickroom — regret your inability to take part in the discussions, and all that, you know. Hire a nurse, if necessary. You might venture to express an opinion or two on vital topics, in my name. I don't care a hang what you say. I only want 'em to think I'm there. No doubt our enemies will have a spy or two hanging about to see that I am actually off for a jaunt with the Rodneys, but they will be Viennese and they won't know me from Adam. What's the odds, so long as Edith is there to stand by you? If she's willing to assume that you are her husband —"

"Good Lord!" half shouted Brock, leaping to his feet,

wide eyed. "You don't mean to say that she is — is — is to go to Vienna with me?"

"Emphatically, yes. She's also invited. Of course, she's going."

"You mean that she's going just as you are going — by proxy?" murmured Brock helplessly.

"Proxy, the devil! 'Pon my soul, Brock, you're downright stupid. She can't have a proxy. They know her. The Rodneys are in some way connections of hers, and all that — third cousins. If she isn't there to vouch for you, how the deuce can you expect to —"

"Medcroft, you *are* crazy! No one but an insane man would submit his wife to — Why, good Lord, man, think of the scandal! She won't have a shred left —"

"At the proper time the matter will be explained to the Rodneys — not at first, you know — and I'll be in a position to step into your shoes before the party returns to Paris. Afterwards the whole trick will be exposed to the world, and she'll be a heroine."

"I'm absolutely paralysed!" mumbled Brock.

"Brace up, old chap. I'm going to take you around to the Ritz at once to introduce you to my wife — to your wife, I might say. She'll be waiting for us, and, take my word for it, she's in for the game. She appreciates its importance. Come now, Brock, it means so little to you, and it means everything to me. You will do this for me? For us?"

For ten minutes Brock protested, his argument growing weaker and weaker as the true humour of the project developed in his mind. He came at last to realise that Medcroft was in earnest, and that the situation was as serious as he pictured it. The Englishman's plea was unusual, but it was not as rattle-brained as it had seemed at the outset. Brock was beginning to see the possibilities that the ruse contained; to say the least, he would be running little or no risk in the event of its miscarriage. In spite of possible unpleasant consequences, there were the elements of a rare lark in the enterprise; he felt himself being skilfully guided past the pitfalls and dangers.

"I shall insist upon talking it over thoroughly with Mrs. Medcroft before consenting," he said in the end. "If she's being bluffed into the game, I'll revoke like a flash. If she's keen for the adventure, I'll go, Rox. But I've got to see her first and talk it all over —"

"'Pon my word, old chap, she's ripping, awfully good sort, even though I say it myself. She's true blue, and she'll do anything for me. You see, Brock," and his voice grew very tender, "she loves me. I'm sure of her. There isn't a nobler wife in the world than mine. Nor a prettier one, either," he concluded, with fine pride in his eyes. "You won't be ashamed of her. You will be proud of the chance to point her out as your wife, take my word for it." Then they set out for the Ritz.

"Roxbury," said Brock soberly, when they were in the Rue de la Paix, after walking two blocks in contemplative silence, "my peace of mind is poised at the brink of an abyss. I have a feeling that I am about to chuck it over."

"Nonsense. You'll buck up when Edith has had a fling at you."

"I suppose I'm to call her Edith."

"Certainly, and I won't mind a 'dear' or two when it seems propitious. It's rather customary, you know, even among the unhappily married. Of course, I've always been opposed to kissing or caressing in public; it's so middle-class."

"And I daresay Mrs. Medcroft will object to it in private," lamented Brock good-naturedly.

"I daresay," said her husband cheerfully. "She's your wife in public only. By the way, you'll have to get used to the name of Roxbury. Don't look around as if you expected to find me standing behind your back when she says, 'Roxbury, dear!' I shan't be there, you know. She'll mean you. Don't forget that."

"Oh, I say," exclaimed Brock, halting abruptly, and staring in dismay at the confident conspirator, "will I have to wear a suit of clothes like that, and an eyeglass, and — and — good Lord! spats?"

"By Jove, you shall wear this very suit!" cried Medcroft, inspired. "We're of a size, and it won't fit you any better than it does me. Our clothes never fit us in London. Clever idea of yours, Brock, to think of it. And, here! We'll stop at this shop and pick up a glass. You can have all day for practice with it. And, I say, Brock, don't you think you can cultivate a — er — little more of an English style of speech? That twang of yours won't —"

"Heavens, man, I'm to be a low comedian, too," gasped Brock, as he was fairly pushed onto the shop. Three minutes later they were on the sidewalk, and Brock was in possession of an object he had scorned most of all things in the world — a monocle.

Arm in arm, they sauntered into the Ritz. Medcroft retained his clasp on his friend's elbow as they went up in the lift, after the fashion of one who fears that his victim is contemplating flight. As they entered the comfortable little sitting-room of the suite, a young woman rose gracefully from the desk at which she had been writing. With perfect composure she smiled and extended her slim hand to the American as he crossed the room with Medcroft's jerky introduction dinging in his ears.

"My old friend Brock, dear. He has consented to be your husband. You've never met your wife, have you, old man?" A blush spread over her exquisite face.

"Oh, Roxbury, how embarrassing! He hasn't even proposed to me. So glad to meet you, Mr. Brock. I've been trying to picture what you would look like, ever since Roxbury went out to find you. Sit here, please, near me.

Roxbury, has Mr. Brock really fallen into your terrible trap? Isn't it the most ridiculous proceeding, Mr. Brock —"

"Call him Roxbury, my dear. He's fully prepared for it. And now let's get down to business. He insists upon talking it over with you. You don't mind me being present, do you, Brock? I daresay I can help you out a bit. I've been married four years."

For an hour the trio discussed the situation from all sides and in all its phases. When Brock arose to take his departure, he was irrevocably committed to the enterprise; he was, moreover, completely enchanted by the vista of harmless fun and sweet adventure that stretched before him. He went away with his head full of the brilliant, quick witted, loyal young American who was entering so heartily into the plot to deceive her own friends for the time being in order that her husband might profit in high places.

"She *is* ripping," he said to Medcroft in the hallway. All of the plans had been made and all of them had been approved by the young wife. She had shown wonderful perspicacity and foresight in the matter of details; her capacity for selection and disposal was even more comprehensive than that of the two men, both of whom were somewhat staggered by the boldness of more than one suggestion which came from her fruitful storehouse of romantic ideas. She had grasped the full humour of the situation, from inception to *dénouement*, and, to all appearance, was heart and soul deep in the venture, despising the risks because she knew that succour was always at her elbow in the shape of her husband's loyal support. There was no condition involved which could not be explained to her credit; adequate compensation for the merry sacrifice was to be had in the brief detachment from rigid English conventionality, in the hazardous injection of quixotism into an otherwise overly healthful life of platitudes. Society had become the sepulchre of youthful inspirations; she welcomed the resurrection. The exquisite delicacy with which she analysed the cost and computed the interest won for her the warmest regard of her husband's friend, fellow conspirator in a plot which involved the subtlest test of loyalty and honour.

"Yes," said Medcroft simply. "You won't have reason to change your opinion, Brock." He hesitated for a moment and then burst out, rather plaintively: "She's an awfully good sort, demme, she is. And so are you, Brock — it's mighty decent of you. You're the only man in all the world that I could or would have asked to do this for me. You are my best friend, Brock — you always have been." He seized the American's hand and wrung it fervently. Their eyes met in a long look of understanding and confidence.

"I'll take good care of her," said Brock quietly.

"I know you will. Good-by, then. I'll see you late this afternoon. You leave this evening at seven-twenty by the Orient Express. I've had the reservations booked and — and —" He hesitated, a wry smile on his lips, "I daresay you won't mind making a pretence of looking after the luggage a bit, will you?"

"I shall take this opportunity to put myself in training against the day when I may be travelling away with a happy bride of my own. By the way, how long am I expected to remain in this state of matrimonial bliss? That's no small detail, you know, even though it escaped for the moment."

"Three weeks."

"Three weeks?" He almost reeled.

"That's a long time in these days of speedy divorces," said Medcroft blandly.

CHAPTER II

THE SISTER-IN-LAW.

The Gare de l'Est was thronged with people when Brock appeared, fully half an hour before departing time. In no little dismay, he found himself wondering if the whole of Paris was going away or, on the other hand, if the rest of the continent was arriving. He felt a fool in Medcroft's unspeakable checked suit; and the eyeglass was a much more obstinate, untractable thing than he had even suspected it could be. The right side of his face was in a condition of semi-paralysis due to the muscular exactions required; he had a sickening fear that the scowl that marked his brow was destined to form a perpetual alliance with the smirk at the corner of his nose, forever destroying the symmetry of his face. If one who has not the proper facial construction will but attempt the feat of holding a monocle in place for unbroken hours, he may come to appreciate at least one of the trials which beset poor Brock.

Every one seemed to be staring at him. He heard more than one American in the scurrying throng say to another, "English," and he felt relieved until an Englishman or two upset his confidence by brutally alluding to him as a "confounded American toady."

It was quite train time before Mrs. Medcroft was seen hurrying in from the carriage way, pursued by a trio of *facteurs*, laden with bags and boxes.

"Don't shake hands," she warned in a quick whisper, as they came together. "I recognised you by the clothes."

"Thank God, it wasn't my face!" he cried. "Are your trunks checked?"

"Yes — this afternoon. I have nothing but the bags. You have the tickets? Then let us get aboard. I just couldn't get here earlier," she whispered guiltily. "We had to say good-by, you know. Poor old Roxy! How he hated it! I sent Burton and O'Brien on ahead of me. My sister brought them here in her carriage, and I daresay they're aboard and abed by this time. You didn't see them? But of course you wouldn't know my maids. How stupid of me! Don't be alarmed. They have their instructions, Roxbury. Doesn't it sound odd to you?"

Brock was icy cold with apprehension as they walked down the line of *wagon-lits* in the wake of the bag-bearers. Mrs. Medcroft was as self-possessed and as *dégagé* as he was ill at ease and awkward. As they ascended the steps of the carriage, she turned back to him and said, with the most malicious twinkle in her eyes —

"I'm not a bit nervous."

"But you've been married so much longer than I have," he responded.

Then came the disposition of the bags and parcels. She calmly directed the porters to put the overflow into the upper berth. The *garde* came up to remonstrate in his most rapid French.

"But where is M'sieur to sleep if the bags go up there?" he argued.

Mrs. Medcroft dropped her toilet bag and turned to Brock with startled eyes, her lips parted. He was standing in the passage, his two bags at his feet, an aroused gleam in his eyes. A deep flush overspread her face; an expression of utter rout succeeded the buoyancy of the moment before.

"Really," she murmured and could go no farther. The loveliest pucker came into her face. Brock waved the *garde* aside.

"It's all right," he explained. "I shan't occupy the — I mean, I'll take one of the other compartments." As the *garde* opened his lips to protest, she drew Brock inside the compartment and closed the door. Mrs. Medcroft was agitated.

"Oh, what a wretched *contretemps!*" she cried in despair. "Roxy has made a frightful mess of it, after all. He has *not* taken a compartment for you. I'm — I'm afraid you'll have to take this one and — and let me go in with —"

"Nonsense!" he broke in. "Nothing of the sort! I'll find a bed, never fear. I daresay there's plenty of room on the train. You shan't sleep with the servants. And don't lie awake blaming poor old Rox. He's lonesome and unhappy, and he —"

"But he has a place to sleep," she lamented. "I'm so sorry, Mr. Brock. It's perfectly horrid, and I'm — I'm dreadfully afraid you won't be able to get a berth. Roxbury tried yesterday for a lower for himself."

"And he — couldn't get one?"

"No, Mr. Brock. But I'll ask the maids to give up their —"

"Please, please don't worry — and please don't call me Mr. Brock. I hate the name. Good night! Now don't think about me. I'll be all right. You'll find me as gay as a lark in the morning."

He did not give her a chance for further protest, but darted out of the compartment. As he closed the door he had the disquieting impression that she was sitting upon the edge of her berth, giggling hysterically.

The *garde* listened to his demand for a separate compartment with the dejection of a capable French attendant who is ever ready with joint commiseration and obduracy. No, he was compelled to inform Monsieur the American (to the dismay of the pseudo-Englishman) it would be impossible to arrange for another compartment. The train was crowded to its capacity. Many had been turned away. No, a louis would not be of avail. The deepest grief and anguish filled his soul to see the predicament of Monsieur, but there was no relief.

Brock's miserable affectation of the English drawl soon

gave way to sharp, emphatic Americanisms. It was after eight o'clock and the train was well under way. The street lamps were getting fewer and fewer, and the soft, fresh air of the suburbs was rushing through the window.

"But, hang it all, I *can't* sit up all night!" growled Brock in exasperated finality.

"Monsieur forgets that he has a berth. It is not the fault of the *compagnie* that he is without a bed. Did not M'sieur book the compartment himself? *Très bien!*"

As the result of strong persuasion, the *garde* consented to make "the grand tour" of the train de luxe in search of a berth. It goes without saying that he was intensely mystified by Brock's incautious remark that he would be satisfied with "an upper if he couldn't do any better." For the life of him, Monsieur the *garde* could not comprehend the situation. He went away, shaking his head and looking at the tickets, as much as to say that an American is never satisfied — not even with the best.

Brock lowered a window-seat in the passage and sat down, staring blankly and blackly out into the whizzing night. The predicament had come upon him so suddenly that he had not until now found the opportunity to analyse it in its entirety. The worst that could come of it, of course, was the poor comfort of a night in a chair. He knew that it was a train of sleeping-coaches — Ah! He suddenly remembered the luggage van! As a last resort, he might find lodging among the trunks!

And then, too, there was something irritating in the suspicion that she had laughed as if it were a huge joke — perhaps, even now, she was doubled up in her narrow couch, stifling the giggle that would not be suppressed.

When the *garde* came back with the lugubrious information that nothing, positively nothing, was to be had, it is painful to record that Brock swore in a manner which won the deepest respect of the trainman.

"At four o'clock in the morning, M'sieur, an old gentleman and his wife will get out at Strassburg, their destination. They are in this carriage and you may take their compartment, if M'sieur will not object to sleeping in a room just vacated by two mourners who today buried a beloved son in Paris. They have kept all of the flowers in their —"

"Four o'clock! Good Lord, what am I to do till then?" groaned Brock, glaring with unmanly hatred at the door of the Medcroft compartment.

"Perhaps Madame may be willing to take the upper —" ventured the guard timorously, but Brock checked him with a peremptory gesture. He proposed, instead, the luggage van, whereupon the guard burst into a psalm of utter dejection. It was against the rules, irrevocably.

"Then I guess I'll have to sit here all night," said Brock faintly. He was forgetting his English.

"If M'sieur will not occupy his own bed, yes," said the guard, shrugging his shoulders and washing his hands of the whole incomprehensible affair. "M'sieur will then be up to receive the Customs officers at the frontier. Perhaps he will give me the keys to Madame's trunks, so that she may not be disturbed."

"Ask her for 'em yourself," growled Brock, after one dazed moment of dismay.

The hours crawled slowly by. He paced the length of the wriggling corridor a hundred times, back and forth; he sat on every window-seat in the carriage; he nodded and dozed and groaned, and laughed at himself in the deepest derision all through the dismal night. Daylight came at four; he saw the sun rise for the first time in his life. He neither enjoyed nor appreciated the novelty. Never had he witnessed anything so mournfully depressing as the first grey tints that crept up to mock him in his vigil; never had he seen anything so ghastly as the soft red glow that suffused the morning sky.

"I'll sleep all day if I ever get into that damned bed," he said to himself, bitterly wistful.

The Customs officers had eyed him suspiciously at the border. They evidently had been told of his strange madness in refusing to occupy the berth he had paid for. Their examination of his effects was more thorough than usual. It may have entered their heads that he was standing guard over the repose of a fair accomplice. They asked so many embarrassing and disconcerting questions that he was devoutly relieved when they passed on, still suspicious.

The train was late, and at five o'clock he was desperately combating an impulse to leave it at Strassburg, find lodging in a hotel, and then, refreshed, set out for London to have it out with the malevolent Medcroft. The disembarking of the venerable mourners, however, restored him to a degree of his peace of mind. After all, he reviewed, it would be cowardly and base to desert a trusting wife; he pictured her as asleep and securely confident in his stanchness. No: he would have it out with Medcroft at some later day.

He was congratulating himself on the acquisition of a bed — although it might possess the odour of a bed of tuberoses — when all of his pleasant calculations were upset by the appearance of a German burgher and his family. It was then that he learned that these people had booked *le compartement* from Strassburg to Munich.

Brock resumed his window-seat and despondently awaited the call to breakfast. He fell sound asleep with his monocle in position; nor did it matter to him that his hat dropped through the window and went scuttling off across the green Rhenish fields. When next he looked at his watch, it was eight o'clock. A small boy was standing at the end of the passage, staring wide eyed at him. Two little girls came piling, half dressed, from a compartment, evidently in response to the youngster's whispered command to hurry out and see the funny man. Brock scowled darkly, and the trio darted swiftly into the compartment.

He dragged his stiff legs into the dining car at Stuttgart and shoved them under a table. The car was quite empty. As he was staring blankly at the menu, the *conducteur* from his car hurried in with the word that Madame would not breakfast until nine. She was still very sleepy. Would Monsieur Medcroft be good enough to order her coffee and rolls brought to her compartment at that hour? And would he mind seeing that the maid saw to it that Raggles surely had his biscuit and a walk at the next station?

"Raggles?" queried Brock, passing his hand over his brow. The other shrugged his shoulders and looked askance. "Oh, yes — I — I understand," murmured the puzzled one, recovering himself. For the next ten minutes he wondered who Raggles could be.

He had eaten his strawberries and was waiting for the eggs and coffee, resentfully eying the early risers who were now coming in for their coffee and rolls. They had slept — he could tell by the complacent manner in which their hair was combed and by the interest they found in the scenery which he had come, by tedious familiarity, to loathe and scorn.

The actions of two young women near the door attracted his attention. From their actions he suddenly gathered that they were discussing him — and in a more or less facetious fashion, at that. They whispered and looked shy and grinned in a most disconcerting manner. He turned red about the ears and began to wonder, fiercely, why his eggs and coffee were so slow in coming. Then, to his consternation, the young women, plainly of the serving-class, bore down upon him with abashed smiles. He noticed for the first time that one of them was carrying a very small child in her arms; as she came alongside, grinning sheepishly, she extended the small one toward the astounded Brock, and said in excellent old English:

"Good morning, Mr. Medcroft." Then, with a rare inspiration, "Baby, kiss papa — come, now."

She pushed the infant almost into Brock's face. He did not observe that it was a beautiful child and that it had a look of terror in its eyes; he only knew that he was glaring wildly at the fiendish nurse, the truth slowly beating its way into his be-addled brain. For a full minute he stared as if petrified. Then, administering a sickly grin, he sought to bring his wits up to the requirements of the extraordinary situation. He lifted his hand and mumbled: "Come, Raggles! I haven't a biscuit, but here, have a roll, do. Give me a — a kiss!" He added the last in most heroic surrender.

The nurse and the maid stared hard at him; the baby turned in affright to cling closely to the neck of the former.

"Good Lord, sir," whispered the nurse, with a nervous glance about her; "this ain't Raggles, sir. *This* is a baby."

"Do you think I'm blind, madam?" whispered he, savagely. "I can see it's a baby, but I didn't know there was to be one. Its father didn't mention it to me."

"It's a wise father that knows his own child," said the nurse, with prompt sarcasm.

"I think they should have prepared me for this," growled he. "Is it supposed to be mine? Does — does Mrs. Medcroft know about it?"

"You mean, about the baby, sir? Of course she does. It's hers. Please don't look so odd, sir. My word, sir, I didn't know you didn't know it, sir. I wasn't told, was I, O'Brien? There, sir, you see! Mrs. Medcroft said as I was to bring Tootles in to you, sir. She said —"

"Tootles?" murmured Brock. "Tootles and Raggles. I daresay there's a distinction without much of a difference. Are you Burton?"

"Yes, Mr. Medcroft. The nurse. Won't you take baby for a minute, sir? Just to get acquainted, and for appearance's sake." She whispered the well-meant entreaty. Brock, now well into the spirit of the situation, obligingly extended his arms. The baby set up a lusty howl of aversion.

"For God's sake, take him back to his mother!" groaned Brock hastily. "He doesn't like strangers! Take him away!"

"It isn't a he, sir," whispered the maid, as the nurse prepared to beat a hasty retreat with the Medcroft offspring. "It's a her, sir."

Brock's face was a study in perplexity as they hurried from the car.

"By George," he muttered, "what next!"

That which did come next was even more amazing than the unexpected advent of Tootles. He barely had recovered his equanimity — with his coffee — when a young lady entered the car. That, of itself, was not much to speak of, but what followed was something that not even he could have dreamed of if he had been given the chance. He afterward recalled, in some distress of mind, that his second quick glance at the newcomer developed into little less than a rude stare of admiration. Small wonder, let it be advanced in his defence.

She was astoundingly fair to look upon — dazzling, it might be said, with some support to the adjective. Moreover, she was looking directly into his eyes from her unstable position near the door; what was more, a shy, even mischievous, smile crept into her face as her glance caught his. Never had he seen a more exquisite face than hers; never had he looked upon a more perfect picture of grace and loveliness and — aye, smartness. She was smiling with unmistakable friendliness and recognition, and yet he could have sworn he had not seen her before in his life. As if he could have forgotten such a face! A sudden sense of enchantment swept over him, indescribable, yet delicious.

She was coming toward him — still smiling shyly, her lips parted as if she were breathing quickly from fear or another emotion. He set down his coffee cup without regard to taste or direction, his gaze fixed upon the trim, slender figure in blue. He now saw that her dark eyes were filled with a soft seriousness that belied her brave smile; a delicate pink had come into her clear, high-bred face; the hesitancy of the gentlewoman enveloped her with a mantle that shielded her from any suspicion of boldness. Brock struggled to his feet, amazement written in his face.

"Good morning, Roxbury," she said, in the most impersonal of greetings. Her smile deepened as the blankness increased in his face. In the most casual, matter-of-fact manner, she appropriated the chair across the table from his. "Please sit down, Roxy."

He sat down abruptly. For a single, tense, abashed moment they looked searchingly into each other's eyes.

"Are you Raggles?" he asked politely.

"You poor man!" she cried, aghast. "Raggles is Edith's French poodle. Has no one told you of the poodle?" She half whispered this. He began to adore her at that very moment — a circumstance well worth remembering.

"No one has told me of *you*, for that matter," he apologised, thrilling with a delight such as he had never known before. "Would you mind whispering to me just who you are? Am I supposed to be your father — or what?"

"It is all so delightfully casual, isn't it?" she said. "I daresay they forgot to tell you that you are a man of family. Didn't they mention me in any way at all?" She pouted very prettily.

"No, they ignored you and Raggles and Tootles. Are there any more in my family that I haven't met?"

"You see, we got to the station quite a bit ahead of Edith. That's how you happened to miss meeting us. We saw you there, however. I recognised you by your clothes. You seemed very unhappy. Oh, I forgot. You wanted to know who I am. Well, I am your sister-in-law." She ordered coffee and toast while he sat there figuring it out. When the waiter departed, he leaned forward and said quite frankly —

"You'll pardon me, I'm sure, but I can't understand how I was so short-sighted as to marry your sister."

"Well, you see, you didn't catch a glimpse of me until after you were married," she railed. "I was in the Sacred Heart convent, you remember."

"Ah, that explains the oversight. I am considered an unusually discriminating person. Let me see: I married a Miss Fowler, didn't I?"

"Yes, Roxbury. Four years ago, in London, at St. George's, in Hanover Square, at four o'clock, on a Saturday. Didn't they tell you all that?"

"I don't think they said anything about it being four o'clock. I'm glad to know the awful details, believe me. Thanks! Do you know I decided you were an American the instant I saw you in the door," he went on, quite irrelevantly.

"How clever of you, Roxbury!"

"Oh, I say, Miss Fowler, I'm not such an ass as I look, really I'm not. I'm trying to look like —"

"'Sh! If you want me to believe you are not the ass you think you look, be careful what you say. Remember I am *not* Miss Fowler to you. I am Constance — sometimes Connie. Can you remember that — Roxbury?"

He drew a long breath. "Oh, I say, Connie, I'd much rather be plain Brock to you."

"Please don't forget that I am doing this for my sister — not for myself, by any manner of means," she said stiffly. He flushed painfully, conscious of the rebuke.

"Please overlook my faults for the time being," he said. "I'll do better. You see, I've been rather overcome by the sense of my own importance. I'm not used to being the head of an establishment. It has dazed me. A great many things have happened to me since I left the Gare de l'Est last night." He was considerate in not referring to his unhappy mode of travelling. "For instance, I've completely lost my head." He might have said hat, but that would have sounded common-place and earthy.

"One does, you know, when he loses his identity," she said sympathetically. "Edith says you are ripping, and all that sort of thing," she went on hurriedly, in perfect mimicry. "You come very highly recommended as a brother-in-law."

"Are you to be with us until the end of the play?"

"Yes. The Rodneys are my friends, not Edith's. Katherine Rodney was in the convent with me. We see a great deal of each other. I'm sure you will like her. Everybody falls dreadfully in love with her."

"How very amiable of you to permit it," he protested gallantly. "I'm sure I shall enjoy falling in love. Which reminds me that I've never had a sister-in-law. They're very nice, I'm told. It's odd that Medcroft didn't tell me about you. Would you mind advancing a bit of general information about yourself — and, I may say, about my family in general? It may come handy."

"I feel as though I had known you for years," she said, frankly returning his gaze. She leaned forward, her elbows on the table, her chin in her hands. "I'm merely Edith's sister. We live in Paris — that is, father and I. I'm three years younger than Edith. Of course, you know how old your wife is, so we won't dwell upon that. You don't? Then I'd demand it of her. I haven't been in Philadelphia since I was seven — and that's ages ago. I have no mother, and father is off in South America on business. So, you see, little sister has to tag after big sister. Oh!" She interrupted the recital with an abrupt change of manner. "I'm so sorry you've finished your coffee. Now you'll have to go. Roxbury always does."

"But I haven't finished," he exclaimed eagerly. "I'm going to have three or four more pots. You have no idea how —"

"It's all right then," she said with her rarest and most confident smile. "Well, Edith asked me to come to London for the season. The Rodneys were in Paris at the time, however, and they had asked me to join them for a fortnight in the Tyrol. When I said that I was off for a visit with the — with you, I mean — they insisted that you all should come too. They are connections, in a way, don't you see. So we accepted. And here we are."

"You don't, by any chance, happen to be engaged to be married, or anything of that sort," he ventured. "Don't crush me! It's only as a safeguard, you know. People may ask questions."

"You are not obliged to answer them, Roxbury," she said. The flush had deepened in her cheek. It convinced him that she *was* in love — and engaged. He experienced a queer sinking of the heart. "You can say that you don't know, if anyone should be so rude as to ask." Suddenly she caught her breath and stared at him in a sort of panic. "Heavens," she whispered, the toast poised halfway to her lips, "*you*'re not, by any chance, engaged, are you? Appalling thought!"

He laughed delightedly. "People won't ask about me, my dear Constance. I'm already married, you know. But if anyone *should* ask, you're not obliged to answer."

She looked troubled and uncertain. "You may be really married, after all," she speculated. "Who knows? Poor old Roxbury wouldn't have had the tact to inquire."

"I am a henpecked bachelor, believe me."

For the next quarter of an hour they chatted in the liveliest, most inconsequential fashion, getting on excellent terms with each other and arriving at a fair sense of appreciation of what lay ahead of them in the shape of peril and adventure.

She was the most delightful person he had ever met, as well as being the most beautiful. There was a sprightly, ever-growing air of self-reliance about her that charmed and reassured him. She possessed the capacity for divining the sane and the ridiculous with splendid discrimination. Moreover, she could jest and be serious with an impartial intelligence that gratified his vanity without in the least inspiring the suspicion that she was merely clever. He became blissfully imbued with the idea that she had surprised herself by the discovery that he was really quite attractive. In fact, he was quite sincerely pleased with himself — for which he may be pardoned if one stops to think how resourceful a woman of tact may be if she is very, very pretty.

And, by way of further analogy, Brock was a thoroughly likable chap, beside being handsome and a thoroughbred to the core. It's not betraying a secret to affirm, cold-bloodedly, that Miss Fowler had not allied herself with the enterprise until after she had pinned Roxbury down to facts concerning Brock's antecedents. She was properly relieved to find that he came of a fine old family and that he had led more than one cotillion in New York.

He experienced a remarkable change of front in respect to Roxbury Medcroft before the breakfast was over. It may have been due to the spell of her eyes or to the call of her voice, but it remains an unchallenged fact that he no longer thought of Medcroft as a stupid bungler; instead, he had come to regard him as a good and irreproachable Samaritan. All of which goes to prove that a divinity shapes our ends, rough hew them how we may.

"I'm sure we shall get on famously," he said, as she signified her desire to return to the compartment. "I've always longed for a nice, agreeable sister-in-law."

"Her mission in life, up to a certain stage, is to make the man appreciate the fact that he has, after all, been snapped up by a small but deserving family," she said blithely. "It is also her duty to pour oil on troubled waters and strew flowers along the connubial highway, so long as her kind offices are not resented. By the way, Roxbury, I am now about to preserve you from bitter reproaches. You have forgotten to order coffee and rolls for your wife."

"Great Scott! So I have! It's nine o'clock." He ordered the coffee and rolls to be sent in at once. "I hope she hasn't starved to death."

"My dear Roxbury," she said sternly, "I must take you under my wing. You have much to accomplish in the next twenty-four hours, not the least of your duties being the subjugation of Tootles and Raggles. Tootles is fifteen months old, it may interest you to know. We can't afford to have Tootles scream with terror every time she sees you, and it would be most unfortunate if Raggles should growl and snap at you as he does at all suspicious strangers. Once in a while he bites too. Do you like babies?"

"Yes, I — I think I do," he said doubtingly. "I daresay I could cultivate a taste for 'em. But, I say," with eager enthusiasm, "I love dogs!"

"It may be distinctly in your favour that Raggles loathes the real Roxbury. He growls every time that Roxy kisses Edith."

"Has he ever bitten Roxy for it?"

"No," dubiously, "but Roxy has had to kick him on several occasions."

"How very tiresome — to kick and kiss at the same time."

"Raggles is very jealous, you understand."

"That's more than I can say for dear old Roxy. But I'll try to anticipate Raggles by compelling Edith to keep her distance," he said, scowling darkly. "Has it not occurred to you that Tootles will be pretty — er — much of a nuisance when it comes to mountain climbing?" He felt his way carefully in saying this.

"Oh, dear me, Roxbury, would you have left the poor

little darling at home — in all that dreadful heat?"

"I'm sure I couldn't have been blamed for leaving her at home," he protested. "She didn't exist until half an hour ago. Heavens! how they do spring up!"

The remainder of Brock's day was spent in getting acquainted with his family — or, rather, his *ménage*. There were habits and foibles, demands and restrictions, that he had to adapt himself to with unvarying benignity. He made a friend of Raggles without half trying; dogs always took to him, he admitted modestly. Tootles was less vulnerable. She howled consistently at each of his first half dozen advances; his courage began to wane with shocking rapidity; his next halfhearted advances were in reality inglorious retreats. Spurred on by the sustaining Constance, he stood by his guns and at last was gratified to see faint signs of surrender. By midday he had conquered. Tootles permitted him to carry her up and down the station platform (she was too young to realise the risk she ran). Edith and Constance, with the beaming nurse and O'Brien, applauded warmly when he returned from his first promenade, bearing Tootles and proudly heeled by Raggles. Fond mothers in the crowd of hurrying travellers found time to look upon him and smile as if to say, "What a nice man!" He could almost hear them saying it. Which, no doubt, accounted for the intense ruddiness of his cheeks.

"Do you ever spank her?" he demanded once of Mrs. Medcroft, after Tootles had brought tears to his eyes with a potent attack upon his nose. She caught the light of danger in his grey eyes and hastily snatched the offending Tootles from his arms.

Miss Fowler kept him constantly at work with his eyeglass and his English, neither of which he was managing well enough to please her critical estimate. In fact, he laboured all day with the persistence, if not the sullenness, of a hard-driven slave. He did not have time to become tired. There was always something new to be done or learned or unlearned: his day was full to overflowing. He was a man of family!

The wife of his bosom was tranquillity itself. She was enjoying herself. When not amusing herself by watching Brock's misfortunes, she was napping or reading or sending out for cool drinks. With all the selfishness of a dutiful wife, she was content to shift responsibilities upon that ever convenient and useful creature — a detached sister.

Brock sent telegrams for her from cities along the way — Ulm, Munich, Salzburg, and others — all meant for the real Roxbury in London, but sent to a fictitious being in Great Russell Street, the same having been agreed upon by at least two of the conspirators. It mattered little that she repeated herself monotonously in regard to the state of health of herself and Tootles. Roxbury would doubtless enjoy the protracted happiness brought on by these despatches, even though they got him out of bed or missed him altogether until they reached him in a bunch the next day. He may also have been gratified to hear from Munich that Roxbury was perfectly lovely. She said, in the course of her longest despatch, that she was so glad that the baby was getting to like her father more and more as the day wore on.

At one station Brock narrowly escaped missing the train. He swung himself aboard as the cars were rolling out of the sheds. As he sank, hot and exhausted, into the seat opposite his wife and her sister, the former looked up from her book, yawning ever so faintly, and asked:

"Are you enjoying your honeymoon, Roxbury?"

"Immensely!" he exclaimed, but not until he had searched for and caught Connie's truant gaze. "Aren't we?" he asked of Miss Fowler, his eyes dancing. She smiled encouragingly.

"I think you are such a nice man to have about," commented Mrs. Medcroft, this time yawning freely and

stretching her fine young arms in the luxury of home con-
tentment.

Brock went to bed early, in Vienna that night — tired but
happy, caring not what the morrow brought forth so long as
it continued to provide him with a sister-in-law and a wife
who was devoted — to another man.

CHAPTER III

THE DISTANT COUSINS.

The end of the week found Brock quite thoroughly domesticated — to use an expression supplied by his new sister-in-law. True, he had gone through some trying ordeals and had lost not a little of his sense of locality, but he was rapidly recovering it as the pathway became easier and less obscure. At first he was irritatingly remiss in answering to the name of Medcroft; but, to justify the stupidity, it is only necessary to say that he had fallen into a condition which scarcely permitted him to know his own name, much less that of another. He was under the spell! Wherefore it did not matter at all what name he went by: he would have answered as readily to one as the other.

He blandly ignored telegrams and letters addressed to Roxbury Medcroft, and once he sat like a lump, with everyone staring at him, when the chairman of the architects' convention asked if Mr. Medcroft had anything to say on the subject under discussion. He was forced, in some confusion, to attribute his heedlessness to a lifelong defect in hearing. Thereafter it was his punishment to have his name and fragments of conversation hurled about in tones so stentorian that he blushed for very shame. In the Bristol, in the Kärntner-Ring, in the Lichtenstein Gallery, in the Gardens — no matter where he went — if he were to be accosted by any of the genial architects it was always in a voice that attracted attention; he could have heard them if they had been a block away. It became a habit with him to instinctively lift his hand to his ear when one of them hove in sight, having seen him first.

"That's what I get for being a liar," he lamented dolefully. Constance had just whispered her condolences. "Do you think they'll consider it odd that you don't shout at me too?"

"You might explain that you can tell what I am saying by looking at my lips," she said. He was immensely relieved.

Considerable difficulty had to be overcome at the Bristol in the matter of rooms. Without going into details, Brock resignedly took the only room left in the crowded hotel — a six by ten cubbyhole on the top floor overlooking the air-shaft. He had to go down one flight for his morning tub, and he never got it because he refused to stand in line and await his turn. Mrs. Medcroft had the choicest room in the otel, looking down upon the beautiful Kärntner-Ring. Constance proposed, in the goodness of her heart, to give up to Brock her own room, adjoining that of her sister, provided Edith would take her in to sleep with her. Edith was perfectly willing, but interposed the sage conclusion that gossiping menials might not appreciate a preference so unique.

Mr. Roxbury Medcroft's sky parlour adjoined the elevator shaft. The head of his bed was in close proximity to the upper mechanism of the lift, a thin wall intervening. A French architect, who had a room hard by, met Brock in the hall, hollow-eyed and haggard, on the morning after their first night. He shouted lugubrious congratulations in Brock's ear, just as if Brock's ear had not been harassed a whole night long by shrieking wheels and rasping cables.

"Monsieur is very fortunate in being so afflicted," he boomed. "A thousand times in the night have I wished that I might be deaf also. Ah, even an affliction such as yours, monsieur, has its benedictions!"

Matters drifted along smoothly, even merrily, for several days. They were all young and full of the joy of living. They laughed in secret over the mishaps and perils; they whiffed and enjoyed the spice that filled the atmosphere in which they lived. They visited the gardens and the Hofs, the Chateau at Schönbrunn, the Imperial stables, the gay "Venice in

Vienna"; they attended the opera and the concerts, ever in a most circumspect "trinity," as Brock had come to classify their parties. Like a dutiful husband, he always included his wife in the expeditions.

"You are not only a most exemplary wife, Mrs. Medcroft," he declared, "but an unusually agreeable chaperon. I don't know how Constance and I could get on without you."

But the day of severest trial was now at hand. The Rodneys were arriving on the fifth day from Berlin. Despite the fact that the Seattle "connections" had never seen the illustrious Medcroft, husband to their distant cousin, there still remained the disturbing fear that they would recognise — or rather fail to recognise him! — from chance pictures that might have come to their notice. Besides, there was always the possibility that they had seen or even met Brock in New York. He lugubriously admitted that he had met unfortunate thousands whom he had promptly forgotten but who seldom failed to remember him. It is not surprising, then, that the Medcrofts, *ex parte*, were in a state of perturbation — a condition which did not relax in the least as the time drew near for the arrival of the five o'clock train from the north. Constance strove faithfully, even valiantly, to inject confidence into the souls of the prime conspirators.

"You have done so beautifully up to this time," she protested to the dolorous Brock, "why should you be afraid? I once read of an Indian chief whose name was Young-Man-Afraid-of-his-Wife! He was a very brave fellow in spite of all that. You are afraid of Edith, but can't you be like the Indian? He —"

"That's all very nice," mourned Brock, "but he could cover his confusion with war paint. Don't forget that, my dear. Think of the difference in our disguises! War paint in daubs versus spats and an eyeglass. Besides, he didn't have to talk West End English. And, moreover, he lived in a wigwam, and didn't have to explain a sky bedroom to strangers who happened along."

"That is a bit awkward," she confessed thoughtfully. "But can't you say that you have insomnia, and can't sleep unless you are above the noise of the street?"

He looked at her with an expression that made a verbal reply to this suggestion altogether unnecessary.

"Nurse says that Tootles has forgotten the real Roxbury," she went on, after a moment. "See how cleverly you have played the part."

Still he stared moodily, unconvinced, at the roadway ahead. They were driving in the Haupt Allee.

"I hope I haven't got Roxbury into trouble by that interview I gave out concerning the new method of fireproofing woodwork in office buildings and hotels. It occurred to me afterward that he is violently opposed to the system. I advocated it. He'll have a — I might say, a devil of a time explaining his change of front."

As a matter of fact, when Medcroft, hiding in London, saw the reproduced interview in the "Times," together with editorial comments upon the extraordinary attitude of a supposedly conservative Englishman of recognised ability, he was tried almost beyond endurance. For the next two or three days the newspapers printed caustic contributions from fellow architects and builders, in each of which the luckless Medcroft was taken to task for advocating an impractical and fatuous New York hobby in the way of construction — something that staid old London would not even tolerate or discuss. The social chroniclings of the Medcrofts in Vienna, as despatched by the correspondents, offset this unhappy "bull" to some extent, in so far as Medcroft's peace of mind was concerned, but nothing could have drawn attention to the fact that he was not in London at that particular time so decisively as the Vienna interview and its undefended front. Even his shrewdest enemy could not have suspected Medcroft of a patience which would permit him to sit quiet in London while the attacks were going on. He found some small solace in the reflection that he could make the end justify the means.

On their return to the Bristol, Brock and Miss Fowler found the fair Edith in a pitiful state of collapse. She declared over and over again that she could not face the Rodneys; it was more than should be expected of her; she was sure that something would go wrong; why, oh, why was it necessary to deceive the Rodneys? Why should they be kept in the dark? Why wasn't Roxbury there to counsel wisely — and more, *ad infinitum*, until the distracted pair were on the point of deserting the cause. She finally dissolved into tears, and would not listen to reason, expostulation, or persuasion. It was then that Brock cruelly but effectively declared his intention to abdicate, as he also had a reputation to preserve. Whereupon, with a fine sense of distinction, she flared up and accused him of treachery to his best friend, Roxbury Medcroft, who was reposing the utmost confidence in his friendship and loyalty. How could she be expected to go on with the play if he, the man upon whom everything depended, was to turn tail in a critical hour like this?

"How can you have the heart to spoil everything?" she cried indignantly. He looked at her in fresh amazement. "Roxbury would never forgive you. We have both placed the utmost confidence in you, Mr. Brock, and —"

"'Sh! Say 'Roxbury, dear'!" interposed the practical Constance. "The walls may have ears, my dears."

Then Mrs. Medcroft plaintively implored his forgiveness, and said that she was miserable and ashamed and very unappreciative. Brock, in deep humility, begged her pardon for his unnecessary harshness, and promised not to offend again.

"The first quarrel," cried Constance delightedly. "How

nicely you've made it up. And you've been married less than a week!"

"Roxbury and I didn't have our first quarrel until we'd been married a year," said Edith reflectively.

"Oh, I say, Edith," exclaimed Brock, with a dark frown, "I'd rather you wouldn't be forever extolling the good qualities of my predecessor. It's very bad taste. Very much like the pies mother used to make."

"Silly!" cried Medcroft's wife, now in fine humour.

"Besides, Rox is an Englishman. It would take him a year to produce a quarrel. The American husband is not so confounded slow. I won't live up to Roxbury in everything."

It was decided that Constance should greet the Rodneys upon their arrival; the Medcrofts were not to appear until dinner time. Afterwards the entire party would attend the opera, which was then in the closing week. Brock, with splendid prodigality, had taken a box for the final performance of "Tristan and Isolde." It is not out of place to remark that Brock loathed the Wagnerian opera; he was of "The Mikado" cult. He took the seats with a definite purpose in mind to cast the burden of responsibility upon his wife, who would be forced to extend herself in the capacity of hostess, giving him the much-needed opportunity to secure safe footing in the dark area of uncertainty. He believed himself capable of diverting the youthful Miss Rodney and his discreet sister-in-law, but he was consumed by an unholy dread of Rodney *père*; something told him that this shrewd American business man was not the kind who would have the wool pulled over his eyes by anyone. Brock felt that the support of Constance was of greater value than that of Edith at any stage or in any emergency.

Besides, he was now quite palpably in love with her! "I've got it bad!" he reflected in sober consideration of his plight. "But," came the ironic justification, "I'm able to confine it to the immediate family. That's more than most husbands can say."

The Rodneys descended upon the Bristol at five o'clock, rushing down from the Nord-Bahnhof as if there was not a minute to spare. Constance pursued Katherine to her room, where they revelled in the delights of a reunion, gradually coming out of its throes as the hour for dressing approached.

"We dine early, dear," said Constance, "with supper after the opera. I must be off to dress."

"I am so eager to meet Mr. Medcroft. Is he nice?"

"He's the dearest thing in the world," cried the other, her cheeks aglow.

"I'm so glad, on Edith's account. Most of these English matches turn out abominably," commented Miss Rodney, who was twenty, very pretty, and very worldly. "Oh, did I tell you that Freddie Ulstervelt is with us?"

"No!"

"We came across him in Berlin, and dad asked him to join us, if he had nothing better to do, so he said he would. He was with us in Dresden and Prague and — don't you think he's awfully jolly?"

"Ripping!" said Constance with deplorable fervour.

"How awfully English! He said he'd seen you in Paris this spring."

"Yes," said Miss Fowler, her cheeks going red suddenly. "I told him you'd asked me to be with you in June." She could have cut out her tongue for saying this, but it was too late. Katherine laughed a trifle hardly after a stiff moment; then a queer light flitted into her eyes — the light of awakened opposition. Constance was saying to herself, "She's in love with Freddie. I might have known it." Back in her brain lay the memory of Freddie's violent protestations of love, uttered during those recent days in Paris. He had threatened to throw himself into the Seine; she remembered that quite well — and also the fact that he did nothing of the sort, but had a very jolly time at Maxim's and sent her flowers by way of repentance. Knowing Freddie so well, it would not have surprised her in the least to find that he had become engaged to Katherine. His heart was a very flexible organ.

"Oh," said Katherine, "I believe he did say that you had mentioned us." Of herself she was asking: "I wonder if she is in love with him!"

And thus it transpired that Freddie Ulstervelt — addle-pated, good-looking, inconstant Freddie, just out of college — was transformed into a bone of contention, whether he would or no.

He was of the kind who love or make love to every new girl they meet, seriously enough at the time, but easily passed over if need be. Rebuffs may have puzzled him, but they left no jagged scar. He belonged to that class which upsets the tranquillity of inexperienced maidens by whispering intensely, "God, it's grand!" And he means it at the moment.

Katherine Rodney was in love with him. He belonged to a fashionable New York family of wealth, and he had been a young lion at Pasadena during the winter just past. He owned automobiles and a yacht and — an extensive wardrobe. These notable assets had much to do with the conquest of Mrs. Rodney: she looked with favour upon the transitory Mr. Ulstervelt, and believed in her heart that he had something to do with the location of the shining sun. But of this affair more anon, as the novelists say.

Brock was presented to the Rodneys just before the party went in to dinner. He managed his eyeglass and his drawl bravely, and got on swimmingly with the elder Rodneys, until Constance appeared with Katherine and Freddie Ulstervelt. It was not until then that it occurred to Miss Fowler that Freddie, being from New York, was almost certain to know Brock either personally or by sight. She experienced a cold chill, the distinct approach of catastrophe. Brock had just been told that young Ulstervelt of New York was to be of the party. His blood ran cold. He had never seen the young man, but he knew his father well; he had even dined at the mansion in Madison Avenue. There was every reason, however, to suspect that Freddie knew him by sight. Even as he was planning a mode of defence in case of recognition, the young man was presented. Brock's drawl was something wonderful.

"I — aw — knew your family, I'm sure — aw, quite sure," he said. "You know, of course, that I lived in your — aw — delightful city for some years. Strange we never met, 'pon my soul."

"Oh, New York's a pretty big place, Mr. Medcroft," said Freddie good-naturedly. He was a slight young fellow with a fresh, inquisitive face. "It's bigger than London in some ways. It's bigger upwards. Say, do you know, you remind me of a fellow I knew in New York!"

"Haw, haw!" laughed Brock, without grace or reason. Miss Fowler caught her breath sharply.

"Fellow named Brock. Stupid sort of chap, my mother says. I —"

"Oh, dear me, Mr. Ulstervelt," cried Edith, breaking in, "you shan't say anything mean about Mr. Brock. He's my husband's best friend."

"I didn't say it, Mrs. Medcroft. It was my mother." Brock was hiding a smile behind his hand. "She knows him better than I. To tell the truth, I've never met him, but I've seen him on the Fifth Avenue stages. You *do* look like him, though, by Jove."

"It's extraordinary how many people think I look like dear old Brock," said the false Roxbury. "But, on the other hand, most people think that Brock looks like me, so what's the odds? Haw, haw! Ripping! Eh, Mr. Rodney?"

"Ripping? Ripping what? Good God, am I ripping anything?" gasped Mr. Rodney, who was fussy and fat and generally futile. He seemed to grow suddenly uncomfortable, as if ripping was a habit with him.

Dinner was a success. Brock shone with a refulgence that bedimmed all expectations. His wife was delighted; in all of the four years of married life, Roxbury had never been so brilliant, so deliciously English (to use her own expression). Constance tingled with pride. Of late, she had experienced unusual difficulty in diverting her gaze from the handsome impostor, and her thoughts were ever of him — in justification of a platonic interest, of course, no more than that. Tonight her eyes and thoughts were for him alone — a circumstance which, could he have felt sure, would have made him wildly happy, instead of inordinately furious in his complete misunderstanding of her manner toward Freddie Ulstervelt, who had no compunction about making love to two girls at the same time. She was never so beautiful, never so vivacious, never so resourceful. Brock was under the spell; he was fascinated; he had to look to himself carefully in order to keep his wits in the prescribed channel.

His self-esteem received a severe shock at the opera. Mrs. Medcroft, with malice aforethought, insisted that Ulstervelt should take her husband's seat. As the box held but six persons, the unfortunate Brock was compelled to shift more or less for himself. Inwardly raging, he suavely assured the party — Freddie in particular — that he would find a seat in the body of the house and would join them during the *Entr'acte*. Then he went out and sat in the foyer. It was fortunate that he hated Wagner. Before the end of the act he was joined by Mr. Rodney, horribly bored and eager for relief. In a nearby *café* they had a whiskey and soda apiece, and, feeling comfortably reinforced, returned to the opera house arm-in-arm, long and short, thin and fat, liberally discoursing upon the intellectuality of Herr Wagner.

"Say, you're not at all like an Englishman," exclaimed

Mr. Rodney impulsively, even gratefully.

"Eh, what?" gasped Brock, replacing his eyeglass. "Oh, I say, now, 'pon my word, haw, haw!"

"You've got an American sense of humour, Medcroft, that's what you have. You recognise the joke that Wagner played on the world. Pardon me for saying it, sir, but I didn't think it was in an Englishman."

"Haw, haw! Ripping, by Jove! No, no! Not you. I mean the joke. But then, you see, it's been so long since Wagner played it that even an Englishman has had time to see the point. Besides, I've lived a bit of my life in America."

"That accounts for it," said the tactless but sincere Mr. Rodney.

Brock glared so venomously at the intrusive Mr. Ulstervelt upon the occasion of his next visit to his own box, that Mrs. Medcroft smiled softly to herself as she turned her face away. A few minutes later she seized the opportunity to whisper in his ear. Her eyes were sparkling, and something in her manner bespoke the bated breath.

"You are in love with my sister," was what she said to him. He blushed convincingly.

"Nonsense!" he managed to reply, but without much persuasiveness.

"But you are. I'm not blind. Anyone can see it. *She* sees it. Haven't you sense enough to hide it from her? How do you expect to win?"

"My dear Mrs. — my dear Edith, you amaze me. I'm confusion itself. But," he went on eagerly, illogically, "do you think I *could* win her?"

"That is not for one's wife to say," she said demurely.

"I'd be tremendously proud of you as a sister-in-law. And I'd be much obliged if you'd help me. But look at that confounded Ulstervelt! He's making love to her with the whole house looking on."

"I think it might be polite if you were to ask him out for a drink," she suggested.

"But I've had one and I never take two."

"Model husband! Then take the girls into the foyer for a stroll and a chat after the act. Don't mind me. I'm your friend."

"Do you think I've got a chance with her?" he asked with a brave effort.

"You've had one wife thrust upon you; why should you expect another without a struggle? I'm afraid you'll have to work for Constance."

"But I have your — I can count on your approval?" he whispered eagerly.

"Don't, Roxbury! People will think you are making love to *me*!" she protested, wilfully ignoring his question.

He returned to the box after the second act and proposed a turn in the foyer. To his disgust, Ulstervelt appropriated Constance and left him to follow with Mrs. Rodney and Katherine. He almost hated Edith for the tantalising smile she shot after him as he moved away, defeated.

If he was glaring luridly at the irrepressible Freddie, he was not alone in his gloom. Katherine Rodney, green with jealousy, was sending spiteful glances after her dearest friend, while Mrs. Rodney was sniffing the air as if it was laden with frost.

"Don't you think Connie is a perfect dear? I'm so fond of her," said Miss Rodney, so sweetly that he should have detected the nether-flow.

He started and pulled himself together. "Aw, yes — ripping!" He consciously adjusted his eyeglass for a hasty glance about in search of the easily disturbed Mr. Rodney. Then, to Mrs. Rodney, his mind a blank after a passing glimpse of Constance and her escort: "Aw — er — a perfectly jolly opera, isn't it?"

CHAPTER IV

THE WOULD-BE BROTHER-IN-LAW.

The next morning, bright and early, Mr. Alfred Rodney, a telegram in his hand, charged down the hall to Mrs. Medcroft's door. With characteristic Far West impulsiveness he banged on the door. A sleepy voice asked who was there.

"It's me — Rodney. Get up. I want to see Medcroft. Say, Roxbury, wake up!"

"Roxbury?" came in shrill tones from within. "He — Isn't he upstairs? Good heaven, Mr. Rodney, what has happened? What *has* happened?"

"Upstairs? What the deuce is he doing upstairs?'"

"He's — he's sleeping! Do tell me what's the matter?"

"Isn't this Mr. Medcroft's room?"

"Ye-es — but he isn't in. He objects to the noise. Oh, has anything happened to Roxbury?" She was standing just inside the door, and her voice betrayed agitation.

"My dear Edith, don't get excited. I have a telegram from —"

She uttered a shriek.

"He's been assassinated! Oh, Roxbury!"

"What the dev — Are you crazy? It's a telegram from —"

"Oh, heavens! I knew they'd kill him — I knew something dreadful would happen if I left —" Here she stopped suddenly. He distinctly heard her catch her breath. After a moment she went on warily: "Is it from a man named Hobart?"

"No! It's from Odell-Carney. Hobart? I don't know anybody named Hobart." (How was he to know that Hobart was the name that Medcroft had chosen for correspondence purposes?) "We're to meet the Odell-Carneys today in Munich. No time to be lost. We've got to catch the nine o'clock train."

"Oh!" came in great relief from the other side of the door. Then, in sudden dismay: "But I can't do it! The idea of getting up at an hour like this!"

"What room is Roxbury in?"

"I — *don't* know!!" in very decided tones. "Inquire at the office!"

Alfred Rodney was a persevering man. It is barely possible that he occupied a lower social plane than that attained by his wife, but he was a man of accomplishment, if not accomplishments. He always did what he set out to do. Be it said in defence of this assertion, he not only routed out his entire protesting flock, but had them at the West-Bahnhof in time to catch the Orient Express — luggage, accessories, and all. Be it also said that he was the only one in the party, save Constance and Tootles, who took to the situation amiably.

"Damn the Odell-Carneys," was what Freddie Ulstervelt said as the train drew out of the station. Brock looked up approvingly.

"That's the first sensible thing I've heard him say," he muttered loud enough to be heard by Miss Fowler. "I say, who are the Odell-Carneys? First I've heard of 'em."

"The Odell-Carneys? Oh, dear, have you never heard of them?" she cried in surprise. He felt properly rebuked. "They are very swell Londoners. It is said —"

"Then, good heavens, they'll know I'm not Medcroft," he whispered in alarm.

"Not at all, my dear Roxbury. That's just where you're wrong. They don't know Roxbury the first. I've gone over it all with Edith. She's just crazy to get into the Odell-Carney set. I regret to say that they have failed to notice the Medcrofts up to this time. Secretly, Edith has ambitions. She has gone to the Lord Mayor's dinners and to the Royal Antiquarians and to Sir John Rodney's and a lot of other functions on the outer rim, but she's never been able to break through the crust and taste the real sweets of London society. My dear Roxbury, the Odell-Carneys entertain the nobility without compunction, and they've been known to hobnob with royalty. Mrs. Odell-Carney was a Lady Somebody-or-other before she married the second time. She's terribly smart, Roxbury."

"How, in the name of heaven, do they happen to be hobnobbing, as you call it, with the Rodneys, may I ask?"

"Well, it seems that Odell-Carney is promoting a new South African mining venture. I have it from Freddie Ulstervelt that he's trying to sell something like a million shares to Mr. Rodney, who has loads of money that came from real mines in the Far West. He'd never be such a fool as to sink a million in South Africa, you know, but he's just clever enough to see the advantage of keeping Odell-Carney in tow, as it were. It means a great deal to Mrs. Rodney, don't you know, Roxbury, to be able to say that she toured with the Odell-Carneys. Freddie says that Cousin Alfred is talking in a very diplomatic manner of going on to London in August to look fully into the master. It is understood that the Rodneys are to be the guests of the Odell-Carneys while in London. It won't be the season, of course, so there won't be much of a commotion in the smart set. It is our dear Edith's desire to slip into the charmed circle through the rift that the Rodneys make. Do you comprehend?"

They were seated side by side in the corner of the compartment, his broad back screening her as much as possible from the persistent glances of Freddie Ulstervelt, who was nobly striving to confine his attentions to Katherine. Brock's eyes were devouring her exquisite face with a greediness that might have caused her some uneasiness if there had not been something pleasantly agreeable in his way of doing it.

"Yes — faintly," he replied, after an almost imperceptible conflict between the senses of sight and hearing. "But how does she intend to explain me away? I'll be a dreadful skeleton in her closet if it comes to that. When she is obliged to produce the real Roxbury, what then?"

"She's thought it all out, Roxbury," said Constance severely but almost inaudibly. "I'm sure Freddie heard part of what you said. Do be careful. She's going to reveal the whole plot to Mrs. Odell-Carney just as soon as Roxbury gives the word — treating it as a very clever and necessary ruse, don't you see. Mrs. Odell-Carney will be implored to aid in the deception for a few days, and she'll consent, because she's really quite a bit of a sport. At the psychological moment the Rodneys will be told. That places Mrs. Odell-Carney in the position of being an abettor or accomplice: she's had the distinction of being a sharer in a most glorious piece of strategy. Don't you see how charmingly it will all work in the end?"

"What are you two whispering about?" demanded Freddie Ulstervelt noisily, patience coming to an end.

"Wha — what the devil is that to —" began Brock furiously. Constance brought him up sharp with a warning kick on the ankle. He vowed afterward that he would carry the mark to his grave.

"He's telling me what a nice chap you are, Freddie," said she sweetly. Brock glared out of the window. Freddie sniffed scornfully.

"I'm getting sick of this job," growled Brock under his breath. "I didn't calculate on —"

"Now, Roxbury dear, don't be a bear," she pleaded so gently, her eyes so full of appeal, that he flushed with sudden shame and contrition.

"Forgive me," he said, the old light coming back into his eyes so strongly that she quivered for an instant before lowering her own. "I hate that confounded puppy," he explained lamely, guarding his voice with a new care. "If you felt as I do, you would too."

She laughed in the old way, but she was not soon to forget that moment when panic was so imminent.

"I — I don't see how anyone can help liking Freddie," she said, without actually knowing why. He stared hard at the Danube below. After a long silence he said —

"It's all tommy-rot about it being blue, isn't it?"

She was also looking at the dark brown, swollen river that has been immortalised in song.

"It's never blue. It's always a yellow-ochre, it seems to me."

He waited a long time before venturing to express the thought that of late had been troubling him seriously.

"I wonder if you truly realise the difficulty Edith will have in satisfying an incredulous world with her absolutely truthful story. She'll have to explain, you know. There's bound to be a sceptic or two, my dear Constance."

"But there's Roxbury," she protested, her face clouding nevertheless. "*He* will set everything right."

"The world will say he is a gullible fool," said he gently. "And the world always laughs at, not with, a fool. Alas, my dear sister, it's a very deep pool we're in." He leaned closer and allowed a quaint, half bantering, wholly diffident smile to cross his face. "I — I'm afraid that you are the only being on earth who can make the story thoroughly plausible."

"I?" she demanded quickly. Their eyes met, and the wonder suddenly left hers. She blushed furiously. "Nonsense!" she said, and abruptly left him to take a seat beside Katherine Rodney. He found small comfort in the whisperings and titterings that came, willy-nilly, to his burning ears from the corner of the compartment. He had a disquieting impression that they were discussing him; it was forced in upon him that being a brother-in-law is not an enviable occupation.

"Wot?" he asked, almost fiercely, after the insistent Freddie had thrice repeated a question.

"I say, will you have a cigaret?" half shouted Freddie, exasperated.

"Oh! No, thanks. The train makes such a beastly racket, don't you know."

"They told me at the Bristol you were deaf, but — Oh, I say, old man, I'm sorry. Which ear is it?"

"The one next to you," replied Brock, recovering from his confusion. "I hear perfectly well with the other one."

"Yes," drawled Freddie, with a wink, "so I've observed." After a reflective silence the young man ventured the interesting conclusion, "She's a stunning girl, all right." Brock looked polite askance. "By Jove, I'm glad she isn't *my* sister-in-law."

"I suppose I'm expected to ask why," frigidly.

"Certainly. Because, if she was, I *couldn't*. Do you get the point?" He crossed his legs and looked insupportably sure of himself.

They reached Munich late in the afternoon and went at once to the Hotel Vier Jahretzeiten, where they were to find the Odell-Carneys.

Mr. Odell-Carney was a middle-aged Englishman of the extremely uninitiative type. He was tall and narrow and distant, far beyond what is commonly accepted as *blasé*; indeed, he was especially slow of speech, even for an Englishman, quite as if it were an everlasting question with him whether it was worth while to speak at all. One had the feeling when listening to Mr. Odell-Carney that he was being favoured beyond words; it took him so long to say anything, that, if one were but moderately bright, he could finish the sentence mentally some little time in advance of the speaker, and thus be prepared to properly appreciate that which otherwise might have puzzled him considerably. It could not be said, however, that Mr. Odell-Carney was ponderous; he was merely the effectual result of delay. Perhaps it is safe to agree with those who knew him best; they maintained that Odell-Carney was a pose, nothing more.

His wife was quite the opposite in nearly every particular, except height and angularity. She was bony and red-faced and opinionated. A few sallow years with a rapid, profligate nobleman had brought her, in widowhood, to a fine sense of appreciation of the slow-going though tiresomely unpractical men of the Odell-Carney type. It mattered little that he made poor investment of the money she had sequestered from his lordship; he had kept her in the foreground by associating himself with every big venture that interested the financial smart set. Notwithstanding the fact that he never was known to have any money, he was looked upon as a financier of the highest order. Which is saying a great deal in these unfeeling days of pounds and shillings.

Of course Mrs. Odell-Carney was dressed as all rangy, long-limbed Englishwomen are prone to dress — after a model peculiarly not her own. She looked ridiculously ungraceful alongside the smart, chic American women, and yet not one of them but would have given her boots to be able to array herself as one of these. There was no denying the fact that Mrs. Odell-Carney was a "regular tip-topper," as Mr. Rodney was only too eager to say. She had the air of a born leader; that is to say, she could be gracious when occasion demanded, without being patronising.

In due course of time the Medcrofts and Miss Fowler were presented to the distinguished couple. This function was necessarily delayed until Odell-Carney had time to go into the details of a particularly annoying episode of the afternoon. He was telling the story to his friend Rodney, and of course everything was at a standstill until he got through.

It seems that Mr. Odell-Carney felt the need of a nap at three o'clock. He gave strict injunctions that there was to be no noise in the halls while he slept, and then went into his room and stretched out. Anyone who has stopped at the Hotel Four Seasons will have no difficulty in recalling the electric hall-bells which serve to attract the chambermaids to given spots. If one needs the chambermaid, he presses the button in his room and a little bell in the hall tinkles furiously until she responds and shuts it off. In that way one is sure that she has heard and is coming, a most admirable bit of German ingenuity. If she happens to be taking her lunch at the time, the bell goes on ringing until she returns; it is a faithful bell. Coming back to Odell-Carney: the maid on his floor was making up a room in close proximity when a most annoying thing happened to her. A porter who had reason to dislike her came along and turned her key from the outside, locking her in the room. She couldn't get out, and she had been warned against making a sound that might disturb the English guest. With rare intelligence, she did not scream or make an outcry, but wisely proceeded to press the button for a chambermaid. Then she evidently sat down to wait. To make the story short, she rang her own call-bell for two hours, no other maid condescending to notice the call, which speaks volumes for the almost martial system of the hotel. The bell was opposite the narrator's door. Is it, therefore, surprising that he required a great deal of time to tell all that he felt? It was not so much of what he did that he spoke at such great length, but of what he felt.

"'Pon me soul," he exploded in the end, twisting his mustache with nervous energy, "it was the demdest nap I ever had. I didn't close my eyes, c'nfend me if I did."

While Odell-Carney was studiously adjusting his eyeglass for a final glare at an unoffending bus boy who almost dropped his tray of plates in consequence, Mr. Rodney fussily intervened and introduced the Medcrofts. Mrs. Odell-Carney was delightfully gracious; she was sure that no nicer party could have been "got together." Her husband may have been excessively slow in most things, but he was quick to recognise and appreciate feminine beauty of face and figure. He unbent at once in the presence of the unmistakably handsome Fowler sisters; his expressive "chawmed" was in direct contrast to his ordinary manner of acknowledging an introduction.

"Mr. Medcroft is the famous architect, you know," explained the anxious Mrs. Rodney.

"Oh, yes, I know," drawled Mr. Odell-Carney. "You American architects are doing great things, 'pon my soul," he added luminously. Brock stuck his eyeglass in tighter and hemmed with raucous precision. Mrs. Medcroft stiffened perceptibly.

"Oh, but he's Mr. Roxbury Medcroft, the great English architect," cried Mrs. Rodney, in some little confusion. Odell-Carney suddenly remembered. He glared hard at Brock; the Rodneys saw signs of disaster.

"Oh, by Jove, are *you* the fellow who put those new windows in the Chaucer Memorial Hall? 'Pon me soul! Are you the man who did that?" There was no mistaking his manner; he was distinctly annoyed.

Brock faced the storm coolly, for his friend Medcroft's sake. "I am Roxbury Medcroft, if that's what you mean, Mr. Odell-Carney."

"I know you're Medcroft, but, hang it all, wot I asked was, did you design those windows? Gad, sir, they're the laughing sensation of the age. Where the devil did you get such ideas — eh, wot?" His wife had calmly, diplomatically intervened.

"I hate that man," said Mrs. Medcroft to her supposed husband a few minutes later. There was a dangerous red in her cheeks, and she was breathing quickly. Brock gave an embarrassed laugh and mentioned something audibly about a "stupid ass."

The entire party left on the following day for Innsbruck,

where Mr. Rodney already had reserved the better part of a whole floor for himself and guests. Mr. Odell-Carney, before they left Munich, brought himself to the point of apologising to Brock for his peppery remarks. He was sorry and all that, and he hoped they'd be friends; but the windows were atrocious, there was no getting around that. His wife smoothed it over with Edith by confiding to her the lamentable truth that poor Odell-Carney hadn't the remotest idea what he was talking about half of the time. After carefully looking Edith over and finding her valuably bright and attractive, she cordially expressed the hope that she would come to see her in London.

"We must know each other better, my dear Mrs. Medcroft," she had said amiably. Edith thought of the famous drawing-rooms in Mayfair and exulted vastly. "And Mr. Medcroft, too. I am so interested in men who have a craft. They always are worth while, really, don't you know. How like an American Mr. Medcroft is. I daresay he gets that from having lived so long with an American wife. And what a darling baby! She's wonderfully like Mr. Medcroft, don't you think? No one could mistake that child's father — never! And, my dear," leaning close with a whimsical air of confidence, "that's more than can be said of certain children I know of in very good families."

Edith may have gasped and looked wildly about in quest of help, but her agitation went unnoticed by the new friend. From that momentous hour Mrs. Medcroft encouraged an inordinate regard for the circumspect. She decided that it was best never to be alone with her husband; the future was now too precious to go unguarded for a single moment that might be unexplainable when the triumphal hour of revelation came to hand. She impressed this fact upon her sister, with the result that while Brock was never alone with his prudent wife, he was seldom far from the side of the adorable lieutenant. As if precociously providing for an ultimate alibi, the fickle Tootles began to show unmistakable signs of aversion for her temporary parent. Mrs. Rodney, being an old-fashioned mother, could not reconcile herself to this unfilial attitude, and gravely confided to her husband that she feared Medcroft was mistreating his child behind their backs.

"Well, the poodle likes him, anyway," protested Mr. Rodney, who liked Brock; "and if a dog likes a man he's not altogether a bad lot. If I were you, I wouldn't spread the report."

"Spread it!" she sniffed indignantly. "Are they not my own cousins? Twice removed," she concluded as an afterthought. "Do you imagine that *I* would spread it? He may be an unnatural father, but I shall not be the one to say so. Please bear that in mind, Alfred."

"Well, let's not argue about it," said Mr. Rodney, departing before she could disobey the injunction.

Of course, there was no little confusion at the Hotel Tyrol when it came to establishing the Medcrofts. For a while it looked as though Brock would have to share a room with Tootles, relegating Burton to an alcove and a couch; but Constance, in a strictly family conclave, was seized by an inspiration which saved the day — or the night, more properly speaking.

"I have it, Roxbury," she cried, her eyes dancing. "You can sleep on the balcony. A great many invalids do, you know."

"But, good heaven, I'm not an invalid," he remonstrated feebly.

"Of course, you're not, but can't you *say* you are? It's quite simple. You sleep in the open air because it does your lungs so much good. Oh, I know! It isn't necessary to expand your chest like that. They're perfectly sound, I daresay. I should think you'd rather enjoy the fresh air. Besides, there isn't a room to be had in the hotel."

"But suppose it should rain!" he protested, knowing full well he was doomed.

"You poor boy, haven't you an umbrella?" she cried with such a perfectly entrancing laugh that he would have slept out in a hailstorm to provide recompense. And so it was settled that he was to sleep in the small balcony just off the baby's luxurious room, the hotel people agreeing to place a cot there at night in order to oblige the unfortunate guest with the affected lung.

"You are so dear and so agreeable, Roxbury," purred Mrs. Medcroft, very much relieved. "If ever I hear of a girl looking for a nice husband, I'll recommend you."

"It's all very nice," said he with a wry grin, "but I'm hanged if I ought to be expected to remember all of my accomplishments." They were sitting in her room, attended by the faithful duenna, Constance. "First, the eyeglass; then the English language, with which I find I'm most unfamiliar; then a deafness in one of my ears — I can't remember which until it's too late; and now I'm to be a tubercular. You've no idea how hard it is for me to speak English against Odell-Carney. I'm an out-and-out amateur beside him. And it's horribly annoying to have Ulstervelt shouting in my ear loud enough for everybody in the dining-room to hear. It's rich, I tell you, and if I didn't love you so devotedly, Edith, I'd be on my way at this very instant. There! I feel better. 'On my way' is the first American line I've had in the farce since we left Stuttgart. By the way, Edith, I'm afraid I'll have to punch Odell-Carney's confounded head before long. He's getting to be so friendly to me as Roxbury Medcroft that I can't endure him as Brock."

"I — I don't understand," murmured Edith plaintively. Constance looked up with a new interest in her ever sprightly face.

"Well, you see, he's working so hard to square himself

with Medcroft for the break he made about the windows, that he's taking his spite out on all American architects. Confound him, he persists in saying I'm all right, but God deliver him from those demmed rotters, the American builders. He says he wouldn't let one of us build a hencoop for him, much less a dog kennel. Oh, I say, Connie, don't laugh! How would you like it if —" But both of them were laughing at him so merrily that he joined them at once. Burton and O'Brien, who had come in, were smiling discreetly.

"Come, Roxbury, what do you say to a good long walk?" cried Constance. "I must talk to you seriously about a great many things, beginning with egotism." He set forth with alacrity, rejoicing in spite of his limitations.

Upon their return from the delightful stroll along the mountain side, she went at once to her room to dress for dinner. Brock, more deeply in love than ever before, lighted a cigar and seated himself in the gallery, dubiously retrospective in his meditations. He was sorely disturbed by her almost constant allusion to Freddie Ulstervelt and his "amazingly attractive ways." Was it possible that she could be really in love with that insignificant little whipper-snapper? He seemed to be propounding this doleful question to the lofty, sphinx-like Waldraster-Spitze, looming dark in the path of the south.

"Hello!" exclaimed a voice close to his ear — the fresh, confident voice that he knew so well. "I've been looking for you everywhere." Freddie drew up a chair and sat down at his "good side." The young man appeared to have something weighty on his mind. Brock shifted uneasily. "I want to put it up to you, Mr. Medcroft, as man to man. You are Connie's brother-in-law and you ought to be able to set me straight."

"Ah, I see," said Brock vaguely.

"You do?" queried the other, surprise and doubt in his

face.

"No, I should say I don't, don't you see," substituted Brock.

"I was wondering how you *could* have seen. It's a matter I haven't discussed with anyone. I've come to have a liking for you, Roxbury. You're my sort; you have a sort of New York feeling about you. I'm sure you're enough of a sport to give me unprejudiced advice. Hands across the sea, see? Well, to get right down to the point, old man — you'll pardon my plain speech — I think Constance ought to marry an American."

Brock sat up very straight. "I think that's — that's a matter for Miss Fowler to determine," he said coldly.

"You don't quite get my meaning," persisted Freddie, crossing his legs comfortably. "I was trying to make it easy for myself."

"You mean, you think she ought to marry you?"

"That's it, precisely. How clever you are."

"But you are said to be engaged to Miss Rodney," ventured Brock, feeling his way.

"That's just the point, Mr. Medcroft. We're not really engaged — but almost. As a matter of fact, we've got to the point where it's really up to me to speak to her father about it, don't you know. Luckily, I haven't."

"Luckily?"

"Yes. That would have committed me, don't you see. I've been tentatively engaged more than a dozen times, but never quite up to the girl's father. Now, I don't mind telling you that I've changed my mind about Katherine. She's a jolly good sort, but she's not just *my* sort. I thought she was, but — well, you know how it is yourself. The heart's a damned queer organ. Mine has gone back to Constance in the last two days. You are her brother-in-law, and you're a good fellow, through and through. I want your help. I've got money to burn, and the family's got position in the States. I can take care of her as she should be taken care of. No little old six-room flat for her. But, of course, you understand, I can't quite carry the thing through with Katherine still feeling herself attached, as it were. The thing to decide is this: how best can I let Katherine down easily and take on Connie without putting myself in a rather hazardous position? I'm a gentleman, you see, and I can't do anything downright rotten. It wouldn't do. I'm sure, in her heart, Connie cares for me. I could make her understand me better if I had half the chance. But a fellow can't get near her nowadays. Don't you think you are carrying the family link too far? Now, what I want to ask of you, as a friend, is this: will you put in a good word for me every chance you get? I'll square myself with Katherine all right. Of course, you'll understand, I don't want to actually break with Katherine until I'm reasonably sure of Constance. I'm a guest of the Rodney family, you see. It would be downright indecent of me. No, sir! I'm not that sort. I shouldn't think of ending it all with Katherine so long as we are both guests of her father. I'd wait until the end of next week."

Brock had listened in utter amazement to the opening portion of this ingenuous proposal. As the flexile youth progressed, amazement gave place to indignation and then to disgust. Brock's brow grew dark; the impulse to pull his countryman's nose was hard to overcome. Never in all his life had he listened to such a frankly cold-blooded argument as that put forth by the insufferable Knicker-bocker. In the end the big New Yorker saw only the laughable side of the little New Yorker's plight. After all, he was a harmless egoist, from whom no girl could expect much in the way of recompense. It mattered little who the girl of the moment might be, she could not hope to or even seek to hold his perambulatory affections. "He's a single example of a great New York class," reflected Brock. "The futile, priggish rich! There are thousands like him in my dear New York — conscienceless, invertebrate, sybaritic sons of idleness, college-bred and under-bred little beasts who can buy and then cast off at their pleasure. They have no means of knowing how to fall in love with a good girl. They have not been trained to it. It is not for their scrambled intellects to discriminate between the chorus-girl brand of attack and the subtle wooing of a gentlewoman. They can't analyse — they can't feel! And this insipid, egotistical little bounder is actually sitting there and asking me to help him with the girl I love! Good Lord, what next?" He surveyed the eager Ulstervelt in the most irritating manner, finally laughing outright in his face. The very thought of him as Connie's accepted lover! She, the adorable, the splendid, the unapproachable! It was excruciatingly funny!

"Oh, I say, old man," cried Freddie, when the disconcerting laugh came, "don't laugh! It's no damned joke."

"'Pon my soul, Ulstervelt," apologised Brock, with a magnanimous smile, "I haven't said it was a joke. You —"

"Then, what are you laughing at? Something you heard yesterday?" with fine scorn. Brock stared hard at the flushed, boyish face of the other; it was weak and yet as hard as brass, hard with the overbearing confidence of the spoiled child of wealth.

"See here, Ulstervelt," he said with sudden coldness, "you're asking my help. That's no way to get it."

"I beg pardon! I don't mean to be rude," apologised Freddie. "But, I say, old man, I'll make it worth your while. My father's got stacks of coin, and he's a power in New York. Odell-Carney's right. American architects can't design good hencoops. What we want in New York is a rattling good, up-to-date Englishman or two to show 'em a few things. They're a lot of muckers over there, take it from me. By Jove, Roxbury, you don't know how I'd appreciate your friendship in this matter. It will simplify things immensely. You'll speak a good word for me when the time comes, now, won't you?"

"You want me to do you a good turn," said Brock slowly. He found himself grinning with a malicious joy. "All right, I'll see to it that Miss Rodney doesn't marry you, my boy. I'll attend to her."

"Just a minute," interrupted Freddie quickly. "Don't be too hasty about that. I want to be sure of Constance first."

"I see. I was just about to add that I'll give Constance a strong hint that one of the most gallant young sparks in New York is likely to propose to her before the end of the week. That will —"

"Heavens!" exclaimed Freddie, in disgust. "You needn't do that. I've already proposed to her five or six times."

"And she — she is undecided?" cried Brock, his eyes darkening.

"No, hang it all, she's *not* undecided. She's said *no* every time. That's why I'm up a tree, so to speak."

"Oh?" was all that Brock said. Of course she couldn't love a creature of Freddie's stamp! He gloated!

"'Gad, you're a lucky dog, Roxbury," went on Freddie enviously. "Money isn't everything. You're married to one of the prettiest and most fascinating women in the world. She's a wonder. You can't blame me for wanting your wife as a sister-in-law. Now, can you? And that kid! You lucky dog!"

CHAPTER V

THE FRIENDS OF THE FAMILY.

Brock discovered in due time that he was living in a lofty but uncertain place, among the clouds of exaltation. It was not until the close of the succeeding day that he began to lower himself grudgingly from the height to which Freddie's ill-mannered confession had led him. By that time he satisfactorily had convinced himself that no one but a fool could have suspected Constance of being in love with Ulstervelt; and yet, on the other hand, was he any better off for this cheerful argument? There was nothing to prove that she cared for him, notwithstanding this agreeable conclusion by contrast. As a matter of fact, he came earthward with a rush, weighted down by the conviction that she did not care a rap for him except as a conveniently moral brother-in-law. He was further distressed by Edith's comfortless, though perhaps well-qualified, announcement that she believed her sister to be in love; she could not imagine with whom; she only knew she "acted as if she were."

"Besides, Roxbury," she said warningly, "it's a most degenerate husband who falls in love with his wife's sister."

They were walking in one of the mountain paths, some distance behind the others. They did not know that Mrs. Odell-Carney had stopped to rest in the leafy niche above the path. She was lazily fanning herself on the stone seat that man had provided as an improvement to nature. Being a sharp-eared person with a London drawing-room instinct, she plainly could hear what they were saying as they approached. These were the first words she fully grasped, and they caused her to prick up her ears:

"I don't give a hang, Edith. I'm tired of being her brother-in-law."

"You're tired of me, Roxbury, that's what it is," in plaintive tones.

"You're happy, you love and are loved, so please don't put it that way. It's not fair. Think of the pitiable position I'm in."

"My dear Roxbury," quite severely, "if there's nothing else that will influence you, just stop to consider the che-ild! There's Tootles, dear Tootles, to think of."

Of course Mrs. Odell-Carney could not be expected to know that Edith was blithely jesting.

"My dear Edith," he said, just as firmly "Tootles has nothing to do with the case. You know, and Constance knows, and I know, and the whole world will soon know that I'm not even related to her, poor little beggar. I don't see why she should come between me and happiness just because she happens to bear a social resemblance to a man who isn't her father. Come, now, let's talk over the situation sensibly."

Just then they passed beyond the hearing of the astonished eavesdropper. Good heaven, what was this? Not his child? Two minutes later Mrs. Odell-Carney was back at the spring where they had left her somnolent husband, who had refused to climb a hill because all of his breath was required to smoke a cigaret.

"Carney," she said sternly, her lips rigid, her eyes set hard upon his face, "how long have the Medcrofts been married?"

He blinked heavily. "How the devil should I know? 'Pon me word, it's —"

"Four years, I think Mrs. Rodney told me. How old is that baby?"

"'Pon me soul, Agatha, I'm as much in the dark as you. I don't know."

"A little over a year, I'd say. Well, I just heard Medcroft say that she wasn't his child. Whose is it?" She stood there like an accusing angel. He started violently, and his jaw dropped; an expression of alarmed protest leaped into his listless eyes.

"'Pon me word, Agatha, how the devil should I know? Don't look at me like that. Give you my word of honour, I don't know the woman. 'Pon me soul, I don't, my dear."

He was very much in earnest, thoroughly aroused by what seemed to be a direct insinuation.

"Oh, don't be stupid," she cried. "Good heavens, can there be a scandal in that lovely woman's life?"

"There's never any scandal in a woman's life unless she's reasonably lovely," remarked he.

"Whose child is she, if she isn't Medcroft's?" she pursued with a perplexed frown.

"Demme, Agatha, don't ask me," he said irritably, passing his hand over his brow. "I've told you that twice. Ask them; I daresay they know."

She looked at him in disgust. "As if I could do such a thing as that! Dear me, I don't understand it at all. Four years married. Yes, I'm sure that's it. Carney, you don't suppose —" She hesitated. It was not necessary to complete the obvious question.

"Agatha," said he, weighing his remark carefully, "I've said all along that Medcroft is a fool. Take those windows, for instance. If he —"

"Oh, rubbish! What have the windows to do with it? You are positively stupid. And I'd come to like her too. Yes, I'd even asked her to come and see me." She was really distressed.

"And why not?" he demanded. "Hang it all, Agatha, it's nothing unusual. She's a jolly good sort and a sight too good for Medcroft. He's a stupid ass. I've said so all along. How the devil she ever married him, I can't see. But, by Jove, Agatha, I can readily see how she might have loved the father of this child, no matter who he is. Take my advice, my dear, and don't be harsh in your judgment. Don't say a word about what you've heard. If they are reconciled to the — er — the situation, why the devil should we give a hang? And, above all, don't let these Rodneys suspect." Here he lowered his voice gradually. "They're a pack of rotters and they couldn't understand. They'd cut her, even if she is a cousin or whatever it is. I've give a year or two of my life to know positively whether Rodney intends taking those shares or not." He said it in contemplative delight in what he would do if it were definitely settled. "I can't stand them much longer."

"What great variety of Americans there are," she reflected. "Mrs. Medcroft and her sister are Americans. Compare them with the Rodneys and Mr. Ulstervelt. No, Carney, I'll not start a scandal. The Rodneys would not understand, as you say. They'd tear her to shreds and gloat over the mutilation. No; we'll have her to see us in London. I like her."

"And, by Jove, Agatha, I like her sister."

"My dear, the baby is a darling."

"But what an ass Medcroft is!"

And thus is it proved that Mrs. Odell-Carney was not only a dutiful wife in taking her husband into her confidence, but also that jointly they enjoyed a peculiarly rational outlook upon the world as they had come to know it and to feel for the people thereof. It is of small consequence that they could not find it in their power to be in tune with the virtuous Rodneys: the Rodneys were conditions, not effects.

However that may be, it was Katherine Rodney, pretty, plump, and spoiled, who pulled the first stone from the foundation of Medcroft's house of cards. Katherine had convinced herself that she was deeply enamoured of the volatile Freddie; the more she thought that she loved him, the greater became the conviction that he did not care as much for her as he professed. She began to detect a decided falling off in his ardour; it was no use trying to hide the fact from herself that Constance was the most disturbing symptom in evidence. Jealousy succeeded speculation. Katherine decided to be hateful; she could not have helped it if she had tried.

It was very evident, to her at least, that Freddie was not to blame; he was being led on by the artful Miss Fowler. There could be no doubt of it — none in the least, declared Miss Rodney in the privacy of her own miserable reflections.

Just as she was on the point of carrying her woes to her mother, an astounding revelation came to her out of a clear sky; an entirely new condition came into the problem. It dawned upon her suddenly, without warning, that Roxbury Medcroft was in love with his sister-in-law!

When she burst in upon her mother, half an hour later, that excellent lady started up from her couch, alarmed by the excitement in her daughter's face. Mrs. Rodney, good soul, was one of the kind who always think the world is coming to an end, or the house is on fire, or the king has been assassinated, if any one approaches with a look of distress in his face.

"My dear, my dear!" she cried, as Katherine stopped tragically in the doorway. "What has happened to your father? Speak!"

"Mamma, it's worse than that! I —"

"Merciful heaven!" The good lady blindly reached for her smelling salts.

"I've made a dreadful discovery," went on Katherine in suppressed tones. "It came to me like a flash. I couldn't believe my own brain. So I watched them from my window. There's no doubt about it, mamma. It's as plain as the nose on your face. He —"

"My darling, what are you talking about? Is my nose — what is the matter with my nose?" She vaguely felt of her nose in horror.

"He's in love with her. There's no mistake. And, will you believe me, mamma, she is *encouraging* him! Positively! Why — why, it's utterly contemptible! Oh, dear, what are we to do?"

Mrs. Rodney looked blankly at her daughter, who had thrown herself in a chair. She gasped and then gave vent to a tremulous squeak.

"In love! Your father? With whom — who is she?"

"Father? Oh, Lord, mother, I didn't say anything about father. Don't cry! It's another man altogether."

"Not Freddie Ulstervelt?" quavered Mrs. Rodney, pulling herself together. "After all he has said to you —"

"No, no, mamma," cried her daughter irritably. "Freddie may be in love with her, but he's not the only one. Mamma!" She straightened up and looked at her mother with wide, horror-struck eyes, "Roxbury Medcroft is madly in love with Constance Fowler!"

Mrs. Rodney did not utter a sound for fully a minute and a half. She never took her eyes from her daughter's distressed face. The colour was coming back into her own, and her lips were setting themselves into thin red lines above her rigid chin.

"I'm sorry, Katherine, that you have seen it too. I have suspected it for several days. But I have not dared to speak — it seemed too improbable. What are we to do?" She sat down suddenly, even weakly.

"She's not only leading Freddie on, but she's flirting with her own brother-in-law — her own sister's husband — her — her —"

"Her own niece's father! It's atrocious!"

"She's a horrid beast! And I *thought* I loved her. Oh, mamma, it's just dreadful!"

"Katherine, control yourself. I will not have you upsetting yourself like this. You'll have another of those awful headaches. Leave it all to me, dear. Something *must* be done. We can't stand by and see dear Edith betrayed. She's so happy and so trusting. And, besides all that, we'd be dragged into the scandal. I —"

"And the Odell-Carneys too. Heavens!"

"It *must* be stopped! I shall go at once to Mrs. Odell-Carney and tell her what we have discovered. It will prepare her. She is the best friend I have, and I know she will suggest a way to put a stop to this thing before it is too late. We must —"

"Why don't you speak to father about it first?"

"Your father! My dear, what would be the use? He wouldn't believe it. He never does. I wonder if dear Mrs. Odell-Carney is in her room." The estimable lady fluttered loosely toward the door. Her daughter called to her.

"If I were you, I'd wait a day or two, mamma." She was quite cool and very calculating now. "It may adjust itself, and — and if we can just drop a hint that we suspect, they won't be so — so — well, so public about it. I *know* — I just *know* that Freddie will be disgusted with her if he sees how she's carrying on." Katherine suddenly had realised that good might spring from evil, after all.

In the mean time, young Mr. Ulstervelt was having troubles and disappointments of his own. Persistent effort to make love to Miss Fowler had finally resulted in an almost peremptory command to desist. An unlucky impulse to hold her hand during one of his attempts to "try her out" met with disaster. Miss Fowler snatched her hand away and, with a look he never forgot, abruptly left him. "It's all off with her," ruminated Freddie, shivering slightly as an after effect of the icy stare she had given him. "She's got it in for me, for some reason or other. Wow! That was a frost! I feel it yet. Medcroft has played the deuce helping me. I wonder if — — Hello! There's Katherine."

Freddie did some rapid-fire thinking in the next half

minute, with the result that Constance Fowler was banished forever from his calculations and Katherine Rodney restored to her own. So long as he could not possibly win Constance he figured that he might just as well devote himself to the girl he was virtually engaged to marry. Freddie's was a convenient and adaptable constancy. Miss Fowler out of sight was also out of mind; he descended upon Katherine with all of the old ardour shining in his eyes. It was soon after Miss Rodney's conference with her mother, and the young lady was off for a walk in the town.

"Hello, Katherine," called he, coming up from behind. "Shopping? Take me along to carry the bundles. I want to begin now."

It was Miss Rodney's fancy to receive his advances with disdain. She assumed a most unfriendly manner.

"Indeed?" with chilling irony. "And why, may I ask?"

Freddie was taken aback. This was most unexpected.

"Practice makes perfect," he said glibly. "Don't you want me to carry 'em, Kitty?" He said it almost tearfully.

Katherine exulted inwardly. Outwardly she was very cool and very baffling. "Please don't call me Kitty. I hate it."

"It's a dear little name. That's what I'm going to call you when we are — well, you know."

"I *don't* know. What are you talking about?"

"Oh, come now, Miss Rodney. Don't be so icy. What's up? Never mind — don't tell me. I know. You're jealous of Connie." It was a bold stroke and it had an immediate effect.

"Jealous!" she scoffed, but her cheeks went red. "Not I, Freddie." She considered for a second and then went on: "She's not in love with you. You must be blind. She's crazy about Mr. Medcroft."

"By Jove," exclaimed Freddie, stopping short, his eyes bulging. He looked at her for a minute in silence, realisation sifting into his face. "You're right! She *is* in love with him. I see it now. Well, what do you think of that! Her brother-in-law!"

"And he is in love with her too. Now you may go back to her and see if you can't win her away from him. I shan't interfere, my dear Freddie. Don't have me on your conscience. Good-by."

She left him standing there in the street. With well-practised tact he darted into a tobacconist's shop.

"Another shake-down," he reflected ruefully. "They're all passing me up today. But, great hooks, what's all this about Medcroft and Constance?" He bought some cigarets and started off for a walk, mildly excited by this new turn of affairs. It occurred to him, as he turned it all over in his mind, that Mrs. Medcroft was amazingly resigned to the situation. Of course, she was not blind to her husband's infatuation for her sister. Therefore, if she were so cheerful and indifferent about it, it followed that she was not especially distressed; in fact, it suddenly dawned upon him she was not only reconciled but relieved. She had ceased to love her husband! She could be a freelance in Love's lists, notwithstanding the inconvenience of a legal attachment. "She's ripping, too," concluded Freddie, with a certain buoyancy of spirit. "If she doesn't love Medcroft, she at least ought to love someone else instead. It's customary. I wonder —" Here he reflected deeply for an instant, his spirits floating high. Then he turned abruptly and made his way to the Tirol.

It came to pass, in the course of the evening, that Mr. Ulstervelt, supremely confident from the effect of past achievements, drew the unsuspecting Mrs. Medcroft into a secluded tête-à-tête. It is not of record that he was ever a diplomatic wooer; one in haste never is. Suffice it to say, Mrs. Medcroft, her cheeks flaming, her eyes wide with indignation, suddenly left the side of the indomitable Freddie and joined the party at the other end of the *entresol*, but not before she had said to him with unmistakable clearness and decision —

"You little wretch! How dare you say such silly things to me!"

The rebuff decisive! And he had only meant to be comforting, not to say self-sacrificing. He'd be hanged if he could understand women nowadays. Not these women, at least. In high dudgeon he stalked from the room. In the door he met Brock.

"For two cents," he declared savagely, as if Brock were to blame, "I'd take the next train for Paris."

Brock watched him down the hall. He drew a handful of small coins from his pocket, ruefully looking them over. "Two cents," he said. "Hang it all, I've nothing here but pfennigs and hellers and centimes."

In the course of his wanderings the disconsolate Freddie came upon Mrs. Odell-Carney and pudgy Mr. Rodney. They were sitting in a quiet corner of the reading-room. Mr. Rodney had had a hard day. He had climbed a mountain — or, more accurately speaking, he had climbed halfway up and then the same half down. He was very tired. Freddie observed from his lonely station that Mr. Rodney was fast dropping to sleep, notwithstanding his companion's rapid flow of small talk. It did not take Freddie long to decide. He was an outcast and a pariah and he was very lonely. He must have someone to talk to. Without more ado he bore down upon the couple, and a moment later was tactfully advising the sleepy Mr. Rodney to take himself off to bed — advice which that gentleman gladly accepted. And so it came about that Freddie sat face to face with the last resort, at the foot of the *chaise-longue*, gazing with serene adulation into the eyes of a woman who might have had a son as old as he — if she had had one at all. She had been a coquette in her salad days; there was no doubt of it. She had encountered fervid gallants in all parts of the world and in all stations of life. But it remained for the gallant Freddie Ulstervelt to bowl her over with surprise for the first time in her long and varied career. At the end of half an hour she pulled herself together and tapped him on the shoulder with her fan, a quizzical smile on her lips.

"My dear Mr. Ulstervelt, are you trying to make love to me? You nice Americans! How gallant you can be. I am quite old enough to be your mother. Believe me, I thank you for the compliment. I can't tell you how I appreciate this delicate flattery. You are very delicious. But," as she arose graciously, "I'd follow Mr. Rodney's example if I were you. I'd go to bed." Then, with a rare smile which could not have been more chilling, she left him standing there.

"By Jove," he muttered, passing his hand across his eyes, as if bewildered, "what was I saying to her? Good Lord, has it got to be a habit with me? Was I making love to — *her*?" He departed for the American bar.

Mrs. Rodney had but little sleep that night. She went to bed in a state of worry and uncertainty, oppressed by the shadows which threatened eternal darkness to the fair name of the family — however distantly removed. Katherine's secret had in reality been news to her; she had not paid enough attention to the Medcrofts to notice anything that they did, so long as they did not do it in conjunction with the Odell-Carneys. The Odell-Carneys were her horizon — morning, noon, and night. And now there was likelihood of that glorious horizon being obscured by a sickening scandal in the vulgar foreground. Inspired by Katherine's dreadful conclusions, the excellent lady set about to observe for herself. During the entire evening she flitted about the hotel and grounds with all the snooping instincts of a Sherlock Holmes. She lurked, if that is not putting it too theatrically. From unexpected nooks she emerged to view the landscape o'er; by devious paths she led her doubts to the gates of absolute certainty, and then sat down to shudder to her heart's content. It was all true! For four hours she had been trying to get to the spot where she could see with her own eyes, and at last she had come to it. Of course, she had to admit to herself that she did not actually hear Mr. Medcroft tell Constance that he loved her, but it was enough for her that he sat with her in the semi-darkness for two unbroken hours, speaking in tones so low that they might just as well have been whispering so far as her taut ears were concerned.

Moreover, other persons than herself had smilingly nudged each other and referred to the couple as lovers; no one seemed to doubt it — nor to resent it, which is proof that the world loves a lover when it recognises him as one.

Mrs. Rodney also discovered that Mrs. Medcroft went to her room at nine o'clock, at least three hours before the subdued tête-à-tête came to an end. The poor thing doubtless was crying her eyes out, decided Mrs. Rodney.

And now, after all this, is it to be considered surprising that the distressed mother of Katherine did not sleep well that night? Nor should her wakefulness be laid at the door of the tired Mr. Rodney, who was ever a firm and stentorian sleeper.

Morning came, and with it a horseback ride for Brock and Miss Fowler. That was enough for Mrs. Rodney; she would hold in no longer. Mrs. Odell-Carney must be told; she, at least, must have the chance to escape before the storm of scandal broke to muddy her immaculate skirts. Forthwith the considerate hostess appeared before her guest with a headful of disclosures. She had decided in advance that it would not do to beat about the bush, so to speak; she would come directly to the obnoxious point.

They were in Mrs. Odell-Carney's sitting-room. Mr. Odell-Carney was smoking a cigaret on the balcony, just outside the window. Mrs. Rodney did not know that he was there. It is only natural that he held himself inhospitably aloof: Mrs. Rodney bored him to death. He did not hear all that was poured out between them, but he heard quite enough to cause him something of a pang. He distinctly heard his wife say things to Mrs. Rodney that she had solemnly avowed she would not say — things about the Medcroft baby.

It goes without saying that Mrs. Odell-Carney refused to be surprised by the disclosures. She calmly admitted that she had suspected Medcroft of being too fond of his sister-in-law, but, she went on cheerfully, why not? His wife didn't care a rap for him — she *said* rap and nothing else; Mrs. Medcroft had an affair of her own, dear child; she was not so slow as Mrs. Rodney thought, oh, no. Mrs. Odell-Carney warmed up considerably in defending the not-to-be-pitied Edith. She said she had liked her from the beginning, and more than ever, now that she had really come to the conclusion that her husband was the kind who sets his wife an example by being a bit divaricating himself.

Mrs. Rodney fairly screeched with horror when she heard that Tootles was "a poor little beggar," and "all that sort of thing, you know."

"My dear," said Mrs. Odell-Carney, hating herself all the time for engaging in the spread of gossip, but femininely unable to withstand the test, "your excellent cousin, Mrs. Medcroft, receives two letters a day from London — great, fat letters which take fifteen minutes to read in spite of the fact that they are written in a perfectly huge hand by a man — a man, d'ye hear? They're not from her husband. He's here. He cannot have written them in London, don't you see? He —"

"I see," inserted Mrs. Rodney, who was afraid that Mrs. Odell-Carney might think she didn't see.

"Mind your Mrs. Rodney, I'm terribly cut up about all this. She has —"

"Oh, I knew you would be," mourned Mrs. Rodney, her heart in her boots. "You must just hate me for exposing you to —"

"Rubbish!" scoffed the other. "It isn't that. I've been through a dozen affairs in which my best friends were frightfully — er — complicated. I meant to say that I'm terribly cut up over poor Mrs. Medcroft. She's a dear. Believe me, she's a most delicious sinner. Even Carney says that, and he's very fastidious — and very loyal."

"They are married in name only," said Mrs. Rodney, beginning to sniffle. She looked up and smiled wanly through her tears. "You know what I mean. My grammar is terrible when I'm nervous." She pulled at her handkerchief for a wavering moment. "Do you think I'd better speak to Edith? We may be able to prevent the divorce."

"Divorce, my dear," gasped Mrs. Odell-Carney incredulously.

At this juncture Mr. Odell-Carney emerged from his shell, so to speak. He stalked through the window and confronted the two ladies, one of whom, at least, was vastly dismayed by his sudden appearance.

"Now, see here," he began without preliminary apology, "I won't hear of a divorce. That's all rubbish — perfect rot, 'pon my soul. Wot's the use? Hang it all, Mrs. Rodney, wot's the odds, so long as all parties are contented? We can stand it, by Jove, if they can, don't you know. We can't regulate the love affairs of the universe. Besides, I'm not going to stand by and see a friend dragged into a thing of this sort —"

"A friend, Carney," exclaimed his wife.

"Well, it's possible, my dear, that he may be a friend. I know so many chaps in London who might be doing this sort of thing, don't you know. Who knows but the chap who's writing her these letters may be one of my best friends? It doesn't pay to take a chance on it. I won't hear to it. If Medcroft knows and his wife knows and Miss Fowler knows, why the deuce should we bother our heads about it? Last night I heard the Medcroft infant bawling its lungs out — teething, I daresay — but did I go in and take a hand in straightening out the poor little beggar? Not I. By the same token, why should I or anybody else presume to step in and try to straighten out the troubles of its parents? It's useless interference, either way you take it."

"I think it's all very entertaining and diverting," said Mrs. Odell-Carney carelessly. She yawned.

"Do you really think so?" asked the doubting Mrs. Rodney. "I was so afraid you'd mind. Your position in society, my dear Mrs. —"

"My position in society, Mrs. Rodney, can weather the tempest you predict," said Mrs. Odell-Carney with a smile that went to Mrs. Rodney's marrow.

"Oh, if — if you really don't mind —" she mumbled apologetically.

"Not at all, my dear madam," remarked Odell-Carney, carefully adjusting his eyeglass. "It's quite immaterial, I assure you."

CHAPTER VI

OTHER RELATIONS.

It is but natural to presume, after the foregoing, that the affairs of the Medcrofts were under close and careful scrutiny from that confidential hour. The Odell-Carneys were conspicuously nice and agreeable to the Medcrofts and Miss Fowler. It may be said, indeed, that Mr. Odell-Carney went considerably out of his way to be agreeable to Mrs. Medcroft; so much so, in fact, that she made it a point to have someone else with her whenever she seemed likely to be left alone with him. The Rodneys struggled bravely and no doubt conscientiously to emulate the example set by the Odell-Carneys, but it was hardly to be expected that they could see new things through old-world eyes. They grew very stiff and ceremonious — that is, the Rodney ladies did. It was their prerogative, of course: were they not cousins of the diseased?

Four or five days of uneasy pretence passed with a swiftness that irritated certain members of the party and a slowness that distressed the others. Days never were so short as those which the now recklessly infatuated Brock was spending. He was valiantly earning his way into the heart of Constance — a process that tried his patience exceedingly, for she was blithely unimpressionable, if one were to judge by the calmness with which she fended off the inevitable though tardy assault. She kept him at arm's length; appearances demanded a discreetness, no matter how she may secretly have felt toward the good-looking husband of her sister. To say that she was enjoying herself would be putting it much too tamely; she was revelling in the fun of the thing. It mattered little to her that people — her own cousins in particular — were looking upon her with cold and critical eyes; she knew, down in her heart, that she could throw a bomb among them at any time by the mere utterance of a single word. It mattered as little that Edith was beginning to chafe miserably under the strain of waiting and deception; the novelty had worn off for the wife of Roxbury; she was despairingly in love, and she was pining for the day to come when she could laugh again with real instead of simulated joyousness.

"Connie, dear," she would lament a dozen times a day, "it's growing unbearable. Oh, how I wish the three weeks were ended. Then I could have my Roxbury, and you could have my other Roxbury, and everybody wouldn't be pitying me and cavilling at you because I'm unhappily married."

"Why do you say I could have your other Roxbury?" demanded her sister on one occasion. "You forget that father expects me to marry the viscount. I —"

"You are so tiresome, Connie. Don't worry me with your love affairs — I don't want to hear them. There's Mr. Brock waiting for you in the garden."

"I know it, my dear. He's been waiting for an hour. I think it is good for him to wait," said the other, with airy confidence. "What does Roxy say in his letter this morning?"

"He says it will all be over in a day or two. Dear me, how I wish it were over now! I can't endure Cousin Mary's snippishness much longer, and as for Katherine! My dear, I hate that girl!"

"She's been very nice lately, Edith — ever since Freddie dropped me so completely. By the way, Burton was telling me today that Odell-Carney had been asking her some very curious and staggering questions about Tootles and your most private affairs."

"I know, my dear," groaned Edith. "He very politely remarked to me last night that Tootles made him think very strangely of a friend of his in London. He wouldn't mention the fellow's name. He only smiled and said, 'Nevah mind, my dear, he's a c'nfended handsome dog.' I daresay he meant that as a compliment for Tootles. She *is* pretty, don't you think so, dear?"

"She's just like you, Edith," said Constance, who understood things quite clearly.

"Then, in heaven's name, Connie, why are they staring at her so impolitely — all of them?"

"It's because she is so pretty. Goodness, Edith, don't let every little thing worry you. You'll have wrinkles and grey hairs soon enough."

"It's all very nice for you to talk," grumbled Edith. "I'm going mad with loneliness. You have a lover near you all the time — he's mad about you. What have I? I'm utterly alone. No one loves me — no, not a soul —"

"You won't let them love you, Edith," said Constance jauntily. "They all want to love you — all of them."

"I hate men," announced Mrs. Medcroft, retrospectively.

Developments of a most refractory character swooped down upon them at the very end of the sojourn in Innsbruck. Every one had begun to rejoice in the fact that the fortnight was almost over, and that they could go their different ways without having anything really regrettable to carry away with them. The Rodneys were going to Paris, the Medcrofts to London, the Odell-Carneys (after finding out where the others were bent) to Ostend. Freddie Ulstervelt suddenly announced his determination to remain at the Tirol for a week or two longer. That very day he had been introduced to a Mademoiselle Le Brun, a fascinating young Parisian, stopping at the Tirol with her mother.

All might have ended well had it not been for the unfortunate circumstance of Odell-Carney's making a purchase of the London *Standard* instead of the *Times*, as was his custom. His lamentations over this piece of stupidity were cut short by the discovery of an astonishing article upon the editorial page of the paper — an article which created within him a sense of grave perplexity. He read the head-lines thrice and glanced through the text twice, neither time with any very definite idea of what he was reading. His fin-gers shook as he held the sheet nearer the window for a final effort to untangle the incredible thing that lay before him in simple, unimpeachable black and white.

"'Pon me word," he kept repeating to himself feebly. Then he got up and went off in extreme haste to find his wife.

"My dear," he said to her in the carriage-way, "I must speak with you alone." She was just starting off for a drive with Mrs. Rodney.

"Bad news, Carney?" she demanded, struck by his ex-pression. She was following him toward a remote corner of the approach. He did not reply until they were seated, much nearer to each other than was their wont.

"Read that," he said, slipping the *Standard* into her hands. "Wot do you think of it?"

"My dear Carney, I don't know. Would you mind telling me what I am to read?"

"The Medcroft thing. Right there."

She read the article, her husband watching her face the while. Surprise, incredulity, dismay, succeeded each other in rapid changes. She was reading in sheer amazement of the doings of Roxbury Medcroft in connection with the County Council's subcommittee — *in London*! The story went on to relate how Medcroft, implacable leader of the opposition to the "grafters," suddenly had appeared before the committee with the most astounding figures and facts to support his charges of rottenness on the part of the "clique"; his unexpected descent upon the scene had thrown the opposing leaders into a panic; every one had been led to believe that he was sojourning in the east. As a matter of fact, it was soon revealed, he had been in London, secretly working on the problem, for nearly three weeks, keeping discreetly under cover in order that his influence might not be thwarted. His array of facts, his bitter arraignment of the men who were trying to force the building bill through the Council, staggered the whole city of London. At that writing it looked as though the bill would be overthrown, its promoters had been so completely put to rout. The committee would be compelled to take cognisance of the startling exposure — the people would demand a full threshing out of the obnoxious deal. Roxbury Medcroft's name was on every one's lips. The *Standard* had profited by securing a great "beat."

The Odell-Carneys looked at each other in wonder and perplexity. "What does it mean?" asked the lady, her eyes narrowing.

"Look here, Agatha, this paper's at least two days old. Now, how the devil can Medcroft be in London and Innsbruck at the same time. He *was* here day before yesterday, wasn't he? I'm so c'nfended unobserving —"

"Yes, yes, he was here. And this paper —" She paused irresolutely.

"Says he was *there*. 'Pon my word, it's most uncanny. There's some mystery here."

"I've got it, Carney! This is not Roxbury Medcroft."

"Good Gawd!"

"This explains everything. Heavens, Carney! This fellow is — is her lover! She's running about the country with him. She's —"

"Her lover? Gad, my dear, he may have been so at one time, but he's the other one's lover now, take my word for it. I say, 'pon my soul, this is a charming game your friends the Rodneys have let us into. They —"

"My friends! Yours, you mean!" she retorted.

"Oh, come now! But let it go at that. They know, of

course, that this fellow isn't her husband, and yet, by Gad, Agatha, they've gone about deliberately palming him off on us as the real article. They are actually sanctioning the whole bloody —"

"Stop a moment, Carney," interrupted his wife. "The London chap may be the fraud. Let us go slow, my dear."

"Slow? How the devil can we go slow in such fast company? No! This fellow is the fraud. And they knew it too. They all know it. They —"

"Rubbish! You forget that the whole Rodney tribe is up in arms because Medcroft is making love to his wife's sister. They're not assuming anything there, let me tell you. And he's not Edith's lover. If he's not her husband, he's playing a part that she understands and approves. And this — this, my dear Carney, may account for the imaginary orphanage of Tootles. Dear me, it's quite a tangle."

"I shall telegraph my solicitors at once for definite news. They'll know whether the real Medcroft is in London, and then — well, by Jove, Agatha, I can't tell just wot steps I'll take in regard to these Rodneys."

He went into a long tirade against the unfortunate Seattle-ites, as he called them. "Understand me, Agatha, I don't blame Mrs. Medcroft. If she's having an affair with this chap and can pull the wool —"

"But she isn't having an affair with this chap," cried Mrs. Odell-Carney, her patience exhausted. "She's having an affair with a chap in London — the one who writes — Good gracious! Of course! Why, what fools we are. The real Medcroft is in London, and it is he who is writing the letters. How stupid of me!"

"Aha!" exclaimed he triumphantly. "Of course, she's getting letters from her husband. Why not? That's to be expected. But, by the everlasting shagpat, do you suppose that her husband knows she's off here with another fellow who masquerades as her husband? No!" He almost shouted it. "I've never heard of anything so brazen. Gad, what nerve these Americans have. Just to think of it!"

"I don't believe she is anything of the sort," declared his wife. "She's as good as gold. You can't fool me, Carney. I know women."

"Deuce take it, Agatha, so do I. And wot's more, I know men."

"They're a poor lot, the kind you know. This pseudo Medcroft is not your kind. He's a very clever chap and a gentleman."

"Now, look here, Agatha, don't imagine that I'm going to be such a cad as to turn against 'em in their hour of trial. Not I. I'm more their friend than ever. I'll help 'em to get away from here, and I'll bulldose these Rodneys into holding their peace forever after. It's the Rodney duplicity that I can't stand."

"Shall we stay here or shall we find an excuse to leave?" she asked pointedly.

"We'll stay long enough for me to tell the Rodneys wot I think of 'em, I'll have an answer to my despatch by night. Then, I should advise you to have a talk with Mrs. Medcroft. You've invited her to the house, you know. Tell her there can't be two Medcrofts. See wot I mean? We'll see 'em through this, but — well, you understand."

Meantime a telegram had preceded a lengthy letter into the department of the police, both directed to Herr Bauer, who in reality was James Githens, of Scotland Yard. The telegram had said: "Why do you say M. is there? He is in London. Explain. Letter tomorrow." The letter had come, and Mr. Githens, as well as the local police office, was "bowled over," to express it in Scotland Yard English. He had wired his employers that "M. is still in Innsbruck. Cannot be in London." It was very clearly set forth in the letter that Roxbury Medcroft was in London, and that Mr. Githens, of Scotland Yard, had betrayed his trust. He was virtually charged with playing into the hands of the enemy — "selling out," as it were. It readily may be expected that Mr. Githens was accused of being in the employ of the "opposition." Moreover, it is but reasonable to assume that he took vigorous steps at once to vindicate himself: which accounts for the woe that lurked close behind the heels of a man named Brock.

Brock and Constance had ridden off that afternoon to visit the historic Schloss Ambras. The great castle had been saved for the very last of their explorations; he had just been able to secure permission to visit that part of the Duke's residence open on certain occasions to the curious public. Edith had declined to accompany them. In the first place, she was expecting the all-important message from her husband — she was "on nettles," to quote her plaintive eagerness; in the second place, she realised that as the crisis was at hand in the affairs of Brock and Constance, her presence was not a necessary adjunct. Not only was she expecting a message from Roxbury, but eagerly anticipating an outburst of joyous news from the two who had, it seemed, very gladly left her behind.

The young couple, returning by the lower road from the Schloss, came to a resting place at a little eating-house and garden on the hillside overlooking the river Inn. It is a quiet, demure, unfrequented place among the crags, standing in from the white roadway a hundred feet or more, clouded by gorgeous trees and sombre cliffs. It was to this charming, romantic retreat that Brock led his fair, now tremulous inamorata. She, too, knew that the hour for decision had come; it was in the air, in the glint of his eyes, in the leaping of her heart. And she knew what she would say to him, and what they would say to the world a few hours hence. The mountains seemed to have lost their splendid frown; they were beaming down upon her, tenderly caressing instead of bleak and foreboding as they always had been before.

A rosy-cheeked girl came into the garden to serve them. Swift, cool breezes were scurrying down the valley, bearing in their wake the soft rain clouds that were soon to drench the earth and then radiantly pass on. They were quite alone, seated in the shelter of a wide, overhanging portico. A soft, green darkness was creeping over the mountainside, pregnant with smell of the shower.

Constance ordered tea and a bite of something to eat for both. Brock's gaze never left her exquisite face while she was engaged in the pretty but rather self-conscious occupation of instructing the waitress. After the girl had departed, he leaned forward across the little table and said, a trifle hoarsely and disjointedly —

"It was most appetising to watch you do that. I could live forever on nothing but tea and sandwiches if you were to order them."

"You've said a great many silly things to me this afternoon."

"I wonder —" he stopped and lowered his voice — "I wonder if you would call it silly if I were to tell you that I love you, very, very much." His gloved hand dropped upon hers as she fumbled aimlessly with the menu card; something in the very helplessness of that long slim hand drew the strength of all his love toward it — all of this confident, arrogant love that had come to be so sure of itself in these last days. His grey eyes, dark with the purpose of his passion, took on a new and impelling glow; she looked into them for an instant, the wavering smile of last resort on her parted lips; then her lids dropped quickly and her lip trembled.

"I should still think you very silly," she said in a very low voice, "unless — unless you *do* love me."

His fingers closed so tightly upon hers that she looked up, her eyes swimming with tenderness. Neither spoke for a long minute, but words were not needed to tell what the soul was saying through the eyes.

"I *do* love you — you know I do, Connie. I've loved you from the first day. I cannot live without you, Connie, darling, you won't keep me waiting? You will be my wife — you will marry me at once? You *do* love me, I know — I've known it for days and days —"

She whimsically broke in upon his passionate declaration, saying with a pretty petulance: "Oh, you have? What insufferable conceit! I —"

He laughed joyously. "I never was so sure of anything in my life," he said. "You couldn't help loving me, Constance; I've loved you so. You don't have to tell me, dear; I know. Still, I'd like to hear you say, with those dear lips as well as with your eyes, that you love me."

She put her hand upon the back of the broad one which held the other imprisoned; there was a proud, earnest light in her eyes. "I *do* love you," she said simply.

"God, but I'm a happy man," he exulted. Forgetful of the time and the place, he half arose and, leaning forward, kissed her full upon the upturned lips.

There was a rattling of chinaware behind them. In no little confusion both came tumbling down from Paradise, and found themselves under the abashed scrutiny of a very red-faced young serving-woman.

"Oh, never mind," stammered Gretchen quite amiably. "I am used to that, madame. A great many ladies and gentlemen come here to — to — what you call it?" She placed the tea and sandwiches before them, her fingers all thumbs, her cheeks aglow.

Brock pulled himself together. Very sternly he said: "This young lady is to be my wife."

"Ach," said Gretchen, with a friendly smile and the utmost deference, "that is what they all say, mein Herr." Then, giggling approvingly, she bustled away.

Brock waited until she was out of sight. "She seems to be onto us, as Freddie would say. But what do we care? I'd like to stand on top of the Bandjoch and shout the news to the world. Wouldn't you, dearest?"

"The world wouldn't hear us, dear," she said coolly. "Besides, it's raining up there. Just look at it sweeping down upon us! Goodness!"

He laughed hilariously, amused by her attempt to be casual and indifferent. "You can't turn it off so easily as that, dearest," he cried. "Come! While it rains we may plan. You will marry me — tomorrow?"

"No!" she cried, aghast. "How utterly ridiculous!"

"Well, then, day after tomorrow?"

"No, no — nor week after next. I —"

"See here, Connie, we've got some one else to consider as well as ourselves. In order to square it all up for Edith, we must be able to say to these people that we haven't been frivolling — that we are going to be married at once. That will let Edith out of the difficulty, and everything will look rosy at the outset. If we put it off, the world will have said things in its ignorance that she can never refute, simply because the world doesn't stop long enough to hear two sides of a story unless they are given pretty closely together. Now Edith is counting on us to put the peeping-Tom Rodneys and the charitable Carneys to rout with our own little bombshell. They're saying nasty things about all of us. They're calling you a vile thing for stealing your sister's husband, and they're calling me a dog for what I'm doing. No telling what they'll be saying if we don't step into the breach as soon as it is opened. We can't afford to wait, no matter what Roxbury says when he comes. We've just got to be able to forestall even dear old Roxbury. Come! Don't you see? We must be married at once."

"Dear me," she murmured softly, "what will papa say?"

"My dear Constance, I will explain it all to your father when he gets back from South America next winter."

It was now raining in torrents. They moved back into

the darkest recess of their shelter, and blissfully looked out upon the drenched universe with eyes that saw nothing but sweet sunshine and fair weather.

The clattering of horses' hoofs upon the hard mountain road sounded suddenly above the hiss of the rain-storm. It was quite dark by this time, night having been hurried on by the lowering skies. A moment later, three horsemen, drenched to the skin, drew up in front of the inn, threw their reins over the posts, and dashed for shelter. They came noisily into the arbour, growling and stamping their soggy feet.

"What, ho!" called one of the newcomers, sticking his head through a window of the house. Brock and Miss Fowler looked on, amused by the plight of the riders. Two of them were unquestionably officers of the police; the third seemed to be an Englishman. They were gruff, burly fellows, all of them. For a few minutes they stormed and growled about their miserable luck in being caught in the downpour, ordering schnapps and brandy in large and instant quantities. At last the Englishman, a heavy, sour-faced man, turned his gaze in the direction of the lovers, who sat quite close together in the dark corner. His gaze developed into a stare, then a look of triumph. A moment later he was pointing out the couple to his companions, all three peering at them with excited eyes.

Brock's face went red under the rude stare; he was on the point of resenting it when the Englishman stepped forward. The American arose at once.

"I've been looking for you, Mr. Medcroft — if that is your name," said the stranger, halting in front of the table. "My name is Githens, Scotland Yard. These men have an order for your arrest. I'd advise you to go with them peaceably. The young woman will not be bothered. She is free to go."

"What are you talking about?" demanded Brock angrily.

Suddenly he felt a chill of misgiving. What had Roxbury Medcroft been doing that he should be subject to arrest?

"You are masquerading here as Roxbury Medcroft the architect. You are not Medcroft. I have watched you for weeks. Today we have learned that Medcroft is in London. Your linen is marked with a letter B. You've drawn money on a letter of credit together with a woman who signs herself as Edith F. Medcroft. There is something wrong with you, Mr. B., and these officers, acting for the hotel and the State Bank, have been instructed to detain you pending an investigation."

Mr. Githens was vindicating himself. He may have been a trifle disconcerted by Miss Fowler's musical laugh and Brock's plain guffaw, but he managed to preserve a stiff dignity. "It's no laughing matter. Officers, this is your man. Take him in charge. Madam, as I understand it, you are the alleged sister of the woman who is working herself off as Mrs. Medcroft. It may interest you to know that your sister — if she is your sister — has locked herself in her room and was in hysterics when I left the hotel. She will be carefully guarded, however. She cannot escape. As for you, madam, there is as yet no complaint against you, but I wish to notify you that you may consider yourself under surveillance until after your friends have had a hearing before the magistrate tomorrow. As soon as it has ceased raining we will ask you to ride with us to the city. As for Mr. B., he is in charge of these officers."

At eight o'clock that evening a solemn cavalcade rode into Innsbruck. There were tears of expostulation in the eyes of the lone young woman, flashes of indignation in those of the tall young man who rode beside her.

The tall young man was going to gaol!

The anti-climax had struck the Hotel Tirol some hours before it came upon Brock and Miss Fowler. It seems that Githens had gone first to the big hostelry in quest of light on the very puzzling dilemma in which he found himself involved. Inquiries at the office only served to stir up a grave commotion among the clerks and managers, all of whom vociferously maintained that the hotel was entirely blameless if any deception had been practised. The Tirol did not tolerate anything that savoured of the scandalous; the Tirol was a respectable house; the Tirol was ever careful, always rigid in the protection of its good name; and so on and so forth at great length and with great precision. But Mr. Githens had two officers with him, and he demanded the person of the man calling himself Roxbury Medcroft. The principal bank in the city was also represented in the company of investigators. Likewise there was a laconic gentleman from the British office.

Mr. Medcroft was out. Then, they agreed, it was necessary to see Mrs. Medcroft, or the lady representing herself to be such. Mr. Githens was permitted to go to her rooms in company with the manager of the hotel. What transpired in those rooms during the next fifteen minutes would be quite impossible to narrate short of an entire volume. Edith promptly collapsed. Subsequently she became hysterical. She begged for time, and, getting it, proceeded to threaten every one with prosecution.

"I *am* Mrs. Medcroft!" she declared piteously. "Where is the American consul? I demand the American consul!"

"What has the American government to do with it?" gruffly demanded Mr. Githens.

"Mr. — Mr. — the gentleman whom you accuse is an American citizen!" she stammered.

"Oho! Then he is not an Englishman?"

"I refuse to answer your questions. You are impertinent. I ask you, sir, as the manager of this hotel, to eject this man from my rooms." The manager smiled blandly and did not eject the man.

"But, madam," he said, "we have a right to know who

and what you are. If Mr. Medcroft is in London, this gentleman surely cannot be he, the real Mr. Medcroft. We must have an explanation."

"I'll — I will explain everything tomorrow. Oh, by the way, is there a telegram for me in the office? There must be. I've been expecting it all day. I telegraphed to London for it."

"There is no telegram down there, madam."

At this juncture Mr. Odell-Carney appeared on the scene, uninvited but welcome.

"Wot's all this?" he demanded sternly. Everybody proceeded at once to tell him. Somehow he got the drift of the story. "Get out — all of you!" he said. "I stand sponsor for Mrs. Medcroft. She *is* Mrs. Medcroft, hang you, sir. If you come around here bothering her again, I'll have the law upon you. The Medcrofts are English citizens and —"

"Oh, they are, are they?" sneered Mr. Githens, with a sinister chuckle.

"Who the devil are you, sir?"

"I'm from Scotland Yard."

"I thought so. You've proved it, 'pon my soul. I am Odell-Carney. Daresay you've heard of me."

"I know you by sight, sir. But that —"

"Clever chap, by Jove! And there's no but about it. Mr. — Mr. — never mind what it is. I don't want to know your name. Mrs. Medcroft, will you permit me to send my wife up to you? Mr. Manager, I insist that you take this c'nfended rabble down to the office and tell them to go to the devil? Don't do it up here; do it down there."

After some further discussion and protest, the Scotland Yard man and his party left the room to its distracted mistress. It may be well to remark, for the sake of local colour, that Tootles was crying lustily, while Raggles barked in spite of all that O'Brien could do to stop him.

Odell-Carney sent his wife to Edith. A few minutes later,

as he was making his way to the office, he came upon Mrs. Rodney and Katherine, hurrying, white-faced, to their rooms.

"Oh, isn't it dreadful?" wailed the former, putting her clenched hands to her temples.

"Isn't wot dreadful?" demanded he brutally.

"About Edith! They're going to arrest her."

"Not if I can help it, madam. Where is Mr. Rodney?"

"He hasn't anything to do with it! We're as innocent as children unborn. It's all shocking to us. Mr. Rodney shouldn't be arrested. His rectitude is without a flaw. For heaven's sake, don't implicate him. He's —"

"Madam, I am not a policeman," said Odell-Carney with scathing dignity. "I want your husband to aid me in hushing this c'nfended thing."

"He shan't do it! I won't permit him to be mixed up in it," almost screamed Mrs. Rodney. "I've just heard that he isn't a husband at all. It's atrocious!"

"Bless me, Mrs. Rodney," roared Odell-Carney, "then you oughtn't to be living with him if he isn't your husband. You're as bad as — Hi, look out, there! Don't do that!" Mrs. Rodney had collapsed into her daughter's arms, gasping for breath.

"She's all upset, Mr. Odell-Carney," said Katherine, shaking her mother soundly. "It's just nerves. If you see papa, send him to us. We must take the *first* train for — for anywhere. Will you tell Mrs. Odell-Carney that if she'll get ready at once, papa will see to the tickets."

"Tickets? But, my dear young lady, we're not going any-where. We're going to stay here and see your cousin out of her troubles. My wife is with her now."

He started away as Mr. Rodney came puffing up the stairs. Odell-Carney changed his mind and waited.

"Where's Edith?" panted Mr. Rodney.

"Good heavens!" groaned his wife, lowering her voice

because three chambermaids were looking on from a near-by turn. "Don't mention that creature's name. Just think what she's got us into. He isn't her husband. Alfred, telephone for tickets on tonight's train. Tomorrow will be too late. I won't stay here another minute. Everybody in the hotel is talking. We'll all be arrested."

But Mr. Rodney, for once, was the head of the family. He faced her sternly.

"Go to your rooms, both of you. We'll stay here until this thing is ended. I don't give a hang what she's done, I'm not going to desert her."

"But — but he isn't her husband," gasped Mrs. Rodney, struck dumb by this amazing rebellion.

"But she's your cousin, isn't she, madam?" he retorted with fierce irony.

"I disown her!" wailed his wife, *sans raison*.

"Go to your rooms!" stormed pudgy Mr. Rodney. Then, as they slunk away, he turned to the approving Odell-Carney, sticking out his chest a trifle in his new-found authority. "I say, Carney, what's to be done next?"

The other looked at him for a moment as if in doubt. Then his face cleared, and he took the little man's arm in his.

"We'll have a drink first and then see," he said.

As they were entering the buffet, a cheery voice accosted them from behind. Freddie Ulstervelt came up, real distress in his face.

"I say, count me in on this. I'll buy, if I may. I've just heard the news from the door porter. Bloody shame, isn't it? I had Mademoiselle Le Brun over to hear the band concert — she is related to that painter woman, by the way; I told Katherine she was. Say, gentlemen, we'll stand by Mrs. Medcroft, won't we? Count me in. If it's anything that money can square, I'm here with a letter of credit six figures long."

"Join us," said Odell-Carney warmly. "You're a good sort, after all."

They sat down at a table. Freddie stood between them, a hand on the shoulder of each. Very seriously he was saying:

"I say, gentlemen, we can't abandon a woman at a time like this. We must stand together. All true sports and black sheep *should* stand together, don't you know."

It is possible that Odell-Carney appreciated the subtlety of this compliment. Not so Mr. Rodney.

"Sports? Black sheep? Upon my soul, sir, I don't understand you," he mumbled. Mr. Rodney, although he hailed from Seattle, had never known anything but a clean and unrumpled conscience.

Freddie clapped him jovially on the shoulder. "It's all right, Mr. Rodney. I'll take your word for it. But if we are black sheep we shan't be blackguards. We'll stand by the ship. What's to be done? Bail 'em out?"

It is of record that the three gentlemen were closeted with the officers and managers for an hour or more, but it is not clear that they transacted anything that could seriously affect the situation.

Mrs. Medcroft, despite Mrs. Odell-Carney's friendly offices, refused point blank to discuss the situation. She did not dare to do or say anything as yet. Her husband had not telegraphed the word releasing her from the sorry compact. She loyally decided to stand by the agreement, no matter what the cost, until she received word from London that he had triumphed or failed in his brave fight against the "bloodsuckers."

"I will explain tomorrow, dear Mrs. Odell-Carney," she pleaded. "Don't press me now. Everything shall be all right. Oh, how I wish Constance were here! She understands. But she's off listening to silly love talk and doesn't even care what happens to me. Burton, will you be good enough to spank Tootles if she doesn't stop that screaming?"

By nine o'clock that night every one was discussing the significant disappearance of Constance Fowler and the fraudulent husband of Mrs. Medcroft. Just as Mr. Odell-Carney was preparing to announce to the unfortunate wife that the couple had eloped in the most cowardly fashion, Miss Fowler herself appeared on the scene, dishevelled, mud-spattered, and hot, but with a look of firm determination in her face. She strode defiantly through the main hall, ignoring the curious gaze of the loungers, whisking the skirt of her habit with disdainful abandon as she passed on to the lift. A few moments later she burst in upon her sister, a very angry young person indeed. The Odell-Carneys were down the hall discussing her strange defection; it was with no little relief that they saw her enter the room.

"Are we alone?" demanded Miss Fowler, not giving Edith time to proclaim her joy at seeing her. "Well, I've arranged a way to get him out," she went on, her lips set.

"Out?" murmured Mrs. Medcroft.

"Of course. We can't let him stay in there all night, Edith. How much money have you? Hurry up, please! Don't stare!"

"In where? Who's in where?"

"He's in gaol!" with supreme scorn. "Haven't you heard?"

Mrs. Medcroft began to cry. "Mr. Brock in gaol? Good heavens, what shall I do? I — I was depending on him so much. He ought to be here at this very instant. What has he been doing?"

"Edith Medcroft, stop sniffling, and don't think of yourself for a while. It will do you a great deal of good. Where's your money?"

Ruthlessly she began to rummage Edith's treasure trunk. The other came to her assistance after a dazed interval. The family purse came to light.

"I have a little over four thousand crowns," she murmured helplessly.

"Give it me, quick. There's no time to waste. I have about five thousand. It's all in notes, thank heaven. It isn't quite enough, but I'll try to make it do. Don't stop me, Edith. I haven't time to answer questions. He's in gaol, didn't you hear me say? And I love him!"

"But the — the money? Is it to bail him out with?"

"Bail? No, my dear, it's to *buy* him out with. Sh! Is there any one in that room? Well, then, I'll tell you something." The heads of the two sisters were quite close together. "He's in a cell at the — the prison-hof, or whatever you call it in German. It's gaol in English. I have arranged to bribe one of the gaolers — his guard. He will let him escape for ten thousand crowns — we must do it, Edith! Then Mr. Brock will ride over the Brenner Pass and catch a train somewhere, before his escape is discovered. I expect to meet him in Paris day after tomorrow. Have you heard from Roxbury?"

"No!" wailed Roxbury's wife.

"He's a brute!" stormed Miss Fowler.

"Constance!" flared Mrs. Medcroft, aghast at this sign of lese-majesty.

"Don't tell anybody," called Constance, as she banged the door behind her.

Soon after midnight a closely veiled lady drove up to a street corner adjacent to the city prison, a dolorous-looking building which loomed up still and menacing just ahead. She alighted and, dismissing the cab, strode off quickly into the side street. At a distant corner, in front of a crowded eating-house, two spirited horses, saddled and in charge of a grumbling stableboy, champed noisily at their bits. The young woman exchanged a few rapid sentences with the boy, and then returned in the direction from which she came. A man stepped out of a doorway as she neared the corner, accosting her with a stealthy deference that proclaimed him to be anything but an unwelcome marauder.

The conversation which passed between the slender, nervous young woman and this burly individual was carried on in very cautious tones, accompanied by many quick and furtive glances in all directions, as if both were in fear of observers. At last, after eager pleading on one side and stolid expostulation on the other, a small package passed from the hand of the young woman into the huge paw of the man. The latter gave her a quick, cautious salute and hurried back toward the gaol.

The veiled young woman, very nervous and strangely agitated, made her way back to the spot where the horses were standing. Making her way through the cluster of small tables which lined the inner side of the sidewalk, she found one unoccupied at the extreme end, a position which commanded a view of the street down which she had just come.

Half an hour passed. Midnight revellers at the surrounding tables began to take notice of this tall, elegant, nervous young woman with the veiled face. It was plain to all of them that she was expecting someone; naturally it would be a man, therefore a lover. Her nervousness grew as the minutes lengthened into the hour. A clock in a tower near by struck one. She was now staring with wide, eager eyes down the street, alertly watching the approach of anyone who came from that direction. Twice she half arose and started forward with a quick sigh of relief, only to sink back again dejectedly upon discovering that she had been mistaken in the identity of a newcomer.

Half past one, then two o'clock. The merry-makers were thinning out; she was quite alone at her end of the place. By this time a close observer might have noticed that she was trembling violently; there was an air of abject fear and despair in her manner.

Why did he not come? What had happened? Had the plot failed? Was he even now lying wounded unto death as the result of his effort to escape captivity? A hundred horrid thoughts raced through her throbbing, overwrought brain. He should have been with her two hours ago — he should now be far on his way to freedom. Alas, something appalling had happened, she was sure of it.

At last there hove in sight, coming from the direction in which lay the prison, a group of three men. It was a jaunty party, evidently under the influence of many libations. They came with arms linked, with dignified but unsteady gait, their hats well back on their heads. In the middle was a very tall man, flanked on one side by a very short fat one, on the other by a slender youth who wanted to sing.

She recognised them and would have drawn back to a less exposed spot, but the slender youth saw her before she could do so. He shouted to his companions as if they were two blocks away.

"There she is! Hooray!"

They bore down upon her. The next instant they were solemnly shaking hands with her, much to her dismay.

"Cons'ance, we've been lookin' f-fer you ever'-where in town. W-where on earth've you been?" asked Mr. Rodney thickly, with a laudable attempt at severity.

"Ever sinch 'leven o'clock, Conshance," supplemented Freddie, trying to frown.

"My dear Miss F-Fowler," began Odell-Carney in, his most suave manner, "it is after two o'clock. In — in the morning at that. You — you shouldn't be sittin' here all 'lone thish — this hour in the morning. Please come home with us. Your mother hash — has ask us to fetch you — I mean your sister. Beg pardon."

"I — I cannot go, gentlemen," she stammered. "Please don't insist — please don't ask why. I cannot go —"

"I shay, Conshance, by Jove, the joke's on you," exclaimed Freddie. "I know who 't ish you're waitin' f-for. Well, he can't come. He's locked in."

"Freddie, you are drunk!" in deep scorn.

"I know it," he admitted cheerfully. "We've looked ever'where for you. We're your frien's. He said it was at 'n eatin'-house. We've been ever' eatin'-house in Inchbrook. Was here first of all. Leave it to Rodney. Wassen we, Rodney? You bet we was. You wassen here at 'leven o'clock. Come on home, Conshance. 'S all right. He's safe. He can't come."

"But he will come, unless something terrible has happened to him," she almost sobbed in her desperation. "Cousin Alfred, *won't* you go to the gaol and see what has happened?"

Mr. Rodney took off his hat gallantly and would have gone to do her bidding had not Mr. Odell-Carney laid a restraining grip upon his shoulder.

"Let me explain, Miss F-Fowler. You shee — see, he told us you'd be here, but, hang it all, you wassen here wh-when we came. Never give up, says I to my frien's. We'll search till doomshday. I knew we'd find you if we kep' on searching. Thash jus' wot I said to Roddy, didn' I, Roddy? We mush have overlokked yo' when we were here at 'leven."

"I was not here at eleven," she cried breathlessly.

"Thash jus' what I tol' 'em," insisted Freddie triumphantly. "I saysh: 'What's use lookin' here? She — she isn't on top of any these tables,' an' I — I knew you wassen unner 'em. You ain't —"

"Permit me," interrupted Odell-Carney with grave dignity. "Your friend, Miss Fowler, is not in gaol. He is out —"

"Not in gaol!" she almost shrieked. "I knew it! I knew it could not go wrong. But where is he?"

"He's out on bail. We bailed him out at half past ten — Wot!" She had leaped to her feet with a short scream and was clutching his arm frantically.

"On bail? At half past ten? Good heavens, then — then — oh, are you sure?"

"Poshtive, abs'lutely."

"Then what has become of my nine thousand crowns?"

"You c'n search me, Conshance," murmured Freddie.

"I don' know what you're talkin' 'bout, Cons'ance," said Mr. Rodney in a very hurt tone. "We — we put up security f'r five thous'n dollars, that's what we did. This is all the thanks we getsh for it. Ungrachful!"

Constance had been thinking very hard, paying no heed to his maudlin defence. It rapidly was dawning upon her that these men had secured her lover's release on bail at half past ten o'clock, an hour and a half before she had given her bribe of nine thousand crowns to the gaoler. That being the case, it was becoming clear to her that the wretch deliberately had taken the money, knowing that Brock was not in the prison, and with the plain design to rob her of the amount. It was a transaction in which he could be perfectly secure; bribing of public officials is a solemn offence in Austria and Germany. She could have no recourse, could make no complaint. Her money was gone!

"Where is Mr. Br — Mr. Medcroft?" she demanded, her voice full of anxiety. If he were out of gaol, why had he failed to come to the meeting-place?

"He's locked in," persisted Freddie.

"That's just it, Miss Fowler," explained Odell-Carney glibly. "You shee — see, it was this way: we got him out on bail on condition he'd 'pear tomorrow morning 'fore the magistrate. Affer we'd got him out, he insisted on coming 'round here so's he could run away with you. That wassen a gennelmanly thing to do, affer we'd put up our money. We coul'n' afford have him runnin' away with you. So we had him locked in a room on top floor of the hotel, where he can't get out 'n' leave us to hold the bag, don't you see. He almos' cried an' said you'd be waitin' at the church or — or something like that bally song, don't you know, an' as a lash reshort, to keep him quiet like a good ferrer — feller, we said we'd come an' get you an' 'splain everything saffis —

sasfac — ahem! sassisfac'rly."

She looked at then with burning eyes. Slow rage was coming to the flaming point; And for this she had sat and suffered for hours in a street restaurant! For this! Her eyes fell upon the limp horses and the dejected stableboy. Two hours!

"You will release him at once!" she stormed. "Do you hear? It is outrageous!"

Without another word to the dazed trio, she rushed to the curb and commanded the boy to assist her into the saddle. He did so, in stupid amazement. Then she instructed him to mount and follow her to the Tirol as fast as he could ride. The horses were tearing off in the darkness a moment later.

The three guardians stood speechless until the clatter died away in the distance. Then Mr. Rodney pulled himself together with an effort and groaned in abject horror.

"By thunner, the damn girl is stealin' somebody's horshes!"

CHAPTER VIII

THE PRODIGAL HUSBAND.

The unlucky Brock, wild with rage and chagrin, had paced his temporary prison in the top storey of the Tirol from eleven o'clock till two, bitterly cursing the fools who were keeping him in durance more vile than that from which they had generously released him. He realised that it would be unwise to create a disturbance in the house by clamouring for freedom, because, in the first place, there already had been scandal enough, and in the second place, his distrustful bondsmen had promised faithfully to seek out the devoted Connie and apprise her of his release. He had no thought, of course, that in the mean time she might be duped into paying a bribe to the guard.

Not only was he direfully cursing the trio, but also the addlepated Medcroft and his own addlepated self. It is to be feared that he had harsh thoughts of all the Medcrofts, as far down as Raggles. His dream of love and happiness had turned into a nightmare; the comedy had become a tragic snarl of all the effects known to melodrama. Bitterly he lamented the fact that now he could not go before the assembled critics in the morning and proclaim to them that Constance was his wife. From this, it readily may be judged that Brock was not familiar with all the details of the vigorous Miss Fowler's plan. As a matter of fact, he did not know that he was expected to fly the country like a fugitive. She had known in her heart that he would never agree to a plan of that sort; it was, therefore, necessary for her to deceive him in more ways than one. Plainly speaking, Brock had laboured under the delusion that she merely proposed to bribe the gaoler into letting him off for the night, in order that by some hook or crook they could be married early in the morning — provided her conception of the State marriage laws as they applied to aliens was absolutely correct. (It was not correct, it may be well to state, although that has nothing to do with the case at this moment.) If he had but known that she contemplated paying ten thousand crowns for his surreptitious release, making herself criminally liable, and that he was expected to catch a night train across the border, it is only just to his manhood to say that he should have balked, even though the act were to cost him years of prison servitude — which, of course, was unlikely in the face of the explanation that would be made in proper time by the real Medcroft. It thus may be seen that Brock not only had been vilely imprisoned twice in the same night, but that he was very much in the dark, notwithstanding his attempt to make light of the situation.

It occurred to him, at two o'clock, that pacing the floor in the agony of suspense was a very useless occupation. He would go to bed. Morning would bring relief and surcease to his troubled mind. Constance was doubtless sound asleep in her room. Everything would have been explained to her long before this hour; she would understand. So, with the return of his old sophistry, he undressed and crawled into the strange bed. Somehow he did not like it as well as the cot in the balcony below.

Just as he was dropping off into the long-delayed slumber, he heard a light tapping at his door. He sat up in bed like a flash, thoroughly wide awake. The rapping was repeated. He called out in cautious tones, asking who was there, at the same time slipping from bed to fumble in the darkness for his clothes.

"'Sh!" came from the hallway. He rushed over and put his ear to the door. "It is I. Are you awake? I can't stay here. It's wrong. Listen: here is a note — under the door. Good night, darling! I'm heartbroken."

"Thank God, it's you!" he cried softly. "How I love you,

Constance!"

"'Sh! Edith is with me! Oh, I wish it were morning and I could see you. I have so much to say."

Another querulous voice broke in: "For heaven's sake, Connie, don't stand here any longer. Our reputations are bad enough as it is. Good night — Roxbury!" He distinctly heard the heartless Edith giggle. Then came the soft, quick swish of garments and the nocturnal visitors were gone. He picked up the envelope and, waiting until they were safely down the hall, turned on the light.

"Dearest," he read, "it was not my fault and I know it was not yours. But, oh, you don't know how I suffered all through those hours of waiting at the café. They did not find me until after two. They were drunk. They tried to explain. What do you think the authorities will do to me if they find that I gave that horrid man bribe money? Really, I'm terribly nervous. But he won't dare say anything, will he? He is as guilty as I, for he took it. He took it knowing that you were free at the time. But we will talk it over tomorrow. I've just got back to the hotel. I wouldn't go to bed until Edith brought me up to hear your dear voice. I am so glad you are not dead. It is impossible to release you tonight. Those wretches have the key. How I loathe them! Edith says the hotel is wild with gossip about *everything* and *everybody*. It's just awful. Be of good heart, my beloved. I will be your faithful slave until death. With love and adoration and kisses. Your own Constance.

"P.S. Roxbury has not made a sign, Edith is frantic."

Several floors below the relieved and ecstatic Brock, Mrs. Medcroft was soon urging her sister to go to bed and let the story go until daylight. She persisted in telling all that she had done and all that she had endured.

"We must never let him know that we actually gave that wretch nearly twenty-five hundred dollars, Edith. He would never forgive us. I admit that I was a fool and a ninny, so don't tell me I am. I can see by the way you are looking that you're just crazy to. It's all Roxbury's fault, anyway. Why should he get up and make a speech in London without letting us know? Just see how it has placed us! I think Mr. Brock is an angel to do what he has done for you and Roxbury. Yes, my dear, you will have to confess that Roxbury is a brute — a perfect brute. I'm sure, if you have a spark of fairness in you, you must hate him. No, no! Don't say anything, Edith. You *know* I'm right."

"I'm not going to say anything," declared Edith angrily. "I'm going to bed."

"Edith, if you don't mind, dear, I think I'll sleep with you." After a moment of deep reflection she added plaintively: "There is so much that I just have to tell you, deary. It — it won't keep till daylight."

Bright and early in the morning, the tired, harassed night-farers were routed from their rooms by a demand from the management of the hotel that they appear forthwith in the private office. This order included every member of Mr. Rodney's party, excepting the Medcroft baby. Considerably distressed and very much concerned over the probable outcome of the conference, the Rodney forces made their way to the offices — not altogether in an open fashion, but by humiliatingly unusual avenues. The Rodney family came down the back stairs. Brock was solemnly ushered through the public office by Mr. Odell-Carney and Freddie Ulstervelt. It is not stretching the truth to say that they were sour and sullen, but, as may be suspected, from peculiarly different causes. At last all were congregated in the stuffy office, very much subdued and very much at odds with each other. Mr. Githens was there. Likewise the gentleman from the bank and a prominent person from the department of police.

Miss Fowler glanced about uneasily, and was relieved to discover that her treacherous gaoler was not there to confront her with charges. It had occurred to her that he might, after all, have tricked her into committing a crime against the government.

It was quite noticeable that Mrs. Rodney and Katherine did not speak to the Medcroft contingent — in fact, they ignored them quite completely. Mrs. Rodney was very pale and very deeply distressed. She cast many glances at the red-eyed and sheepish Mr. Rodney — glances that meant much to the further torture of his soul.

"I am sorry to inform you, Herr Rodney, that the rooms which you now occupy, and those of your friends, are no longer at your disposal. They have been engaged for from sometime this day by a —"

"Look here," interrupted Odell-Carney bluntly, "if you mean that we are not wanted here any longer, why not say so? Don't lie about it. We are leaving today, in any event, so wot's the odds? Now, come down to facts: why are we summoned here like a crowd of school children?"

The manager looked at Mr. Githens and then at the police officer.

"Ahem! It seems that Herr Grabetz of the police department desires to ask some questions of your party in my presence. You will understand, sir, that the hotel has been imposed upon by — by these people. It seems, also, that the bank insists upon having some light thrown upon the methods by which Mrs. Medcroft secures money on her letter of credit."

"You are welcome to all that, sir," declared Mr. Odell-Carney, "but I am interested to know just why my wife and I are brought into this affair."

"Because you are guests of Mr. Rodney, sir, I regret to state. We have no complaint against you, sir. *You* are well known here. The — the others are not. They are — what you call it? Humbugs! It may be that they also have swindled you!"

Mr. Rodney, at this point, leaped to his feet and rushed over to shake his fist in the face of the insulting hotel man. But Edith Medcroft arose suddenly, like a tragedy queen, and spoke, her clear, determined voice stilling the turbulent spirit of her outraged host.

"One moment, please," she said. "This all can be satisfactorily explained. No wrong has been done. It will all be cleared up in time. We —"

"In time?" interrupted the manager. "Madam, *this* is the time. You are here with a man who is not your husband, yet who purports to be such."

"It may throw some light on the matter if I announce that the gentleman in question is *my* affianced husband." It was Miss Fowler who spoke. Every one stared at her as she moved over to Brock's side.

"If you will look in the office, you will find a telegram there for me," went on Mrs. Medcroft, pale but absolutely confident. The manager called out through the door. Absolute silence reigned while the reply was awaited.

"No telegram for Mrs. Medcroft last night or today," announced the manager sternly, as he glanced through the slim bunch of blue envelopes. "There are four here for a Mr. Brock, who has not yet arrived in —"

"Brock!" shouted three voices in one.

A tall man, forgetting his English and his eyeglass, sprang forward and grabbed the telegrams from the manager's hand. "Holy mackerel! Give 'em here!" he shouted. Two eager, beautiful young women were hanging to his elbows as he ruthlessly broke one of the seals. "The chump! It's from Rox! They're all from Rox — and they are two or three days old!"

Just then the unexpected happened.

The office door opened with a bang, and the real Roxbury Medcroft stepped into the room. He halted just inside the door and looked about in momentary bewilderment.

"This is a private —" began the manager, stepping forward. A flying figure sped past him; a delighted little shriek rang in his ears. He saw Edith Medcroft hurl herself into the arms of her own husband. At the same moment Brock bounded across the room and pounced eagerly upon the welcome intruder.

"Good Gawd!" gasped Odell-Carney. "Wot's all this?" His wife suddenly began fanning herself, searching for breath.

"*This* is my husband!" cried Edith, triumph in her voice, tears in her eyes, as she faced the astonished observers. "Now, what have you to say?"

It was a perfectly natural but not an especially obvious question. The little manager threw up his hands and cried out in a sad mixture of French, English and Helvetian —

"What? Another husband? Madam, how many more do you propose to inflict us with? We cannot allow it! The management will not permit you to change husbands the instant a new guest arrives in the house. It is not to be heard of — no, no!"

"Are you afraid that the books won't balance?" asked Brock with a joyous grin, a great load off his heart. "Ladies and gentlemen, permit me to introduce Mr. Roxbury Medcroft, my friend and fellow conspirator. He is the husband of this lady, not I. I am to be the husband of *this* lady, thank God."

There was a moment of absolute silence — it may have been stupor. The two audiences faced each other with emotions widely at variance. It was Mrs. Rodney who spoke first.

"Is this true, Edith?" she quavered.

"Yes, yes, yes!" cried Edith, her eyes dancing.

"Then, what are you doing here with a man who isn't your husband?" demanded Mrs. Rodney, suddenly aflame.

"I can explain everything to you later on, Mrs. Rodney,"

interposed Mrs. Odell-Carney calmly. She had divined at least a portion of the truth, and she was clever enough to put herself on the right side. Edith cast an involuntary look of surprise at the Englishwoman. "I have known everything from the first. Mrs. Medcroft and I are closer friends than you may have thought." She gave Edith a meaning look, and a moment later was whispering to her in a private corner of the private office: "My dear, I don't know what it means, but you must tell me everything as soon as possible. I am your friend. Whatever it all is, it's ripping!"

There was a great deal of pow-wowing and chatter, charges and refutations, excuses and explanations. Mr. Medcroft finally waved every one aside in the most *dégagé* manner imaginable.

"Don't crowd me! Hang it all, I'm not a curiosity. There isn't anything to go crazy about. My friend, Mr. Brock, has just done me a trifling favour. That's all. The whole story will be in the London papers this morning. Buy 'em. I'm going up to my wife's room to see my baby. I'll come down and explain everything when I've had a bit of a breathing spell. It's annoying to have had this fuss about a simple little matter of generosity on the part of my friend, who, I've no doubt, has been a most exemplary husband. I'll see to it, by Gad, that he receives the proper apologies. And, for that matter, my wife may have something to say about the outrage that has been perpetrated."

He took it all very much as if the world owed him an explanation and not *vice versa*. As he was stalking from the room, Brock bethought himself to ask —

"When did you arrive, old man?"

"Last night on the 12.10. I registered as Smith. It was so late that I decided not to disturb Edith. They said in the office that you'd gone to bed, Brock. Now that I recall it, they said it in a very odd way too. In fact, one of the clerks asked if I had it in for you too."

"You were here all night?" murmured Constance in plaintive misery.

"Well, not precisely all night, Connie. Half of it," replied Roxbury. "Brock, you ass, I telegraphed you I was coming and asked you to meet me at the station. I telegraphed twice from London and —"

"Don't call me an ass," grated Brock. "Why didn't you send 'em to me as Medcroft? I haven't been Brock until this very morning."

"'Pon my soul, Brock, it was rather stupid of me," he confessed sheepishly. "But, you see," with an inspired smile, "one of 'em was to congratulate you on winning Connie. By Jove, you know, I *couldn't* very well address that one to myself."

"But — but he hadn't won me," stammered Constance Fowler.

"Edith," said Roxbury, deep reproach in his voice, "you wrote me that a week ago!" Edith merely squeezed his arm.

Odell-Carney came forward and extended his hand. "Permit me to introduce myself, sir. I am George Odell-Carney. It has given me great pleasure to serve you without knowing you. In my catalogue of personalities you have posed intermittently as a demmed bounder, a deceived husband, a betrayed lover, a successful lover, and a lot of other things I can't just now recall. Acting on the presumption that you might have been a friend in distress, I worked hard in your interest. Now I discover, to my gratification, you are a perfect stranger whom I am proud to meet. Permit me to offer my warmest felicitations and to assure you that Mr. Brock will make a splendid brother-in-law." He hesitated a moment and then went on: "So *you* are the chap that really put in those c'nfended memorial windows. 'Pon me word, sir, they are the rottenest —"

"Carney!" came the sharp reminder from his wife.

"I should have said," revised Mr. Odell-Carney, "you are

the chap who played the deuce with the building grafters in the County Council. Remarkable!"

"Yes," said Roxbury, striving to grasp something of the situation as it appeared to the other. "We beat them. The bill is lost. It will never go to the Council. The subcommittee will not recommend it. Thanks, Brock, old man; you have saved London a good many millions, I daresay. It was you who did it, after all."

Before noon the hotel was agog with the full details of the remarkable story. Cabled despatches in the newspapers gave the gist of the clever trick played by the Medcrofts, and the whole of England was to ring with the stories of Mrs. Medcroft's pluck and devotion. Everybody was buying the papers and staring with admiration at Mrs. Medcroft.

The management of the Tirol implored the Medcrofts to remain — forever! The bank and the police were profuse in apologies and explanations, and Mr. Githens departed by the first train.

Freddie Ulstervelt, killing two birds with one stone, arranged a splendid dinner for that night in honour of the prodigal husband of Edith and also in open compliment to the vivacious Mademoiselle Le Brun.

Later in the day, it occurred to him that he might just as well kill three birds as two, so he planned to announce the betrothal of Miss Fowler and Mr. Brock, the wedding to take place a fortnight hence in Mayfair. The Rodneys were invited to "stop over" for the spread. It is left for the reader to supply the answer to this simple question —

Did they stop over?

THE END

www.ingramcontent.com/pod-product-compliance
Lightning Source LLC
Chambersburg PA
CBHW020152180626
46810CB00004B/1863